GO WITH GRACE

SELENA BAILEY #4

H.K. CHRISTIE

If you would like to use material from this book, prior written permission must be obtained by contacting the publisher at:

www.authorhkchristie.com

First edition: March 2021

ISBN: 978-1-953268-01-3

1

TAYLOR

Supply. Demand. Is there anything more dull than economics? No, but at least I have him to look at. His perfect face. His kind eyes. His broad shoulders. It was worth the temporary torture of an early morning class and the dreadful subject.

He tapped furiously on the keyboard of his laptop, no doubt taking notes on the lecture. He was focused. Dedicated. Driven. It was what I loved most about him.

I took a sip from my water bottle and thought back to the first time I'd seen his beautiful face.

The air was warm with a light breeze as I strolled down to the middle of campus to visit the booths at the Volunteer Fair. Flipping through pamphlets at the Green Peace booth, I glanced up and spotted him a few tables down at the Amnesty International table. I didn't know his name or his story, but I knew I had to know more. I thanked the crunchy-granola types for their time before hurrying off to shadow his steps through the quad. He stopped at a table one stall down from the Italian Club, where I planted myself and pretended to be interested in the club while I studied him speaking to a representative from the Freshman Orientation Group.

He raked his fingers through his dark hair before giving that killer smile and bending over to scribble on a piece of paper attached to a clipboard. I casually stumbled over to him, gently bumping into him. I apologized profusely, claiming I was a clumsy goof. He laughed off the entire incident before asking if I was interested in signing up to help with the Fall Freshman Orientation. He said it was the least that I could do since I'd practically mauled him.

The light hit his face and his eyes twinkled as he chuckled at his own quip. No, I didn't have any interest in orienting new freshman and wasn't eligible considering I was an incoming freshman myself, but I was deeply interested in getting to know *him* better. Within moments, I agreed and filled out the sign-up sheet with phony contact information. A tiny white lie didn't hurt anyone, right? I was about to engage further when he peered at the screen of his phone before glancing back up at me. "Ugh. I'm late. Again." He grinned and said, "I guess I'll be seeing you at orientation - hey, try to not mow down any unsuspecting victims before then, okay?"

I chortled, "I'll do my best." As he hurried off, my insides tingled. I watched him until he was out of sight before turning my attention to the sign-up sheet burning his name and email address into my memory.

I spent the rest of my summer imagining what our next encounter would be like. I must have tried on two thousand outfits and rehearsed our next meeting in front of the mirror a dozen times. I wondered if I should play hard to get and pretend to not remember him, or if I should be bold and ask him out for coffee. So many scenarios.

When the day finally came, my nerves were in overdrive. I showed up twenty minutes early to make sure I would be in his group. I paced the halls until he finally arrived. He opened the door to the student union building and our eyes met. *Recognition.* He tipped his chin and said, "Hey there! I know you."

My body melted at the sound of his voice. I asked how the rest of his summer was, but before he could answer, the first of the students arrived. *No biggie.* We had all afternoon and the rest of our lives.

He and I spent the next three hours exploring the campus with the other freshman. When his focus wasn't on the other students, sparks flew between us as he engaged me in small talk and told funny anecdotes about his own first year of college. He hadn't even batted an eye when I confessed I was actually a freshman. My heart nearly caught on fire when he flashed a toothy grin and the sun beamed on his tan face, causing his blue eyes to twinkle. He'd said, "That makes sense, you seemed to hesitate when I asked you to sign up to help. It's good to see you again."

My entire body flushed with anticipation of what was to come next. Would he ask me out? Would we have any classes together? It wasn't likely since he was a senior and I was a freshman, but when genuine love was at play, anything was possible. To my dismay, at the end of orientation, he was once again in a hurry, but before he could run off I stared into his eyes. "What a day. It was fun, right?"

"Yeah, it was cool."

"Maybe we could grab coffee sometime?" I asked, having decided on a bold approach.

He gave me an adorable lopsided grin. "Sounds great. Why don't you put your number in my phone?" He handed me his cell phone, and I typed in my name and number. I finished and slid it back into his hand.

"Thanks. Gotta jam. I'll see you later."

I wore a silly grin as I waved goodbye.

The next hours and days were torture. I hadn't heard from him. Not even a text. I figured he must have been busy getting ready for his last year of college. When the fall semester started and I still hadn't heard from him, I realized I needed to take matters into my own hands. It was easy enough. Well, easy enough once I cozied up to one of the student workers in the admissions office — that's how I got a copy of his class schedule. After that, I simply signed up for the same economics course he was enrolled in.

Sure, I had to change my major to take the class, but it was worth it. He was worth it. It would all be worth it. It was as if I could see our entire future together like a television show. Like one of those silly romantic comedies where you know she likes him and he doesn't realize it, but then he has an epiphany that his future wife was right in front of him the whole time. I didn't fault him for not recognizing genuine love. Boys could be a little slow in matters of the heart. I could be patient, but it wouldn't hurt if I helped the process along. What man wouldn't be flattered by a secret admirer? Before long he'd be intensely curious about me; then I'd reveal my identity and our story would begin. A simple, but important plan.

I KICKED MYSELF OUT OF THE MEMORY AND WATCHED HIM like a movie. He appeared to hang onto every word the stuffy old professor, wearing tweed and khaki, muttered. I wondered if our kids would get his serious side or his dark hair or my fair skin. Of course, we'd wait until after we both graduated and settled into our careers, but it would happen. I could feel it in my soul — the two of us were meant to be together.

The professor finally finished his lecture, and I shut my notebook and bent over to stuff it into my backpack. I zipped it shut and glanced back over to my angel. My heartbeat sped up.

Who the *hell* is that?

He was already in the aisle of the lecture hall talking to *that* girl.

I hadn't noticed her in class before. She seemed oddly dressed, in all black with piercings up the ridge of her ear. She wasn't Dillon's type at all. I was his type. Feminine. Soft. Loving. Adoring. So, why was he talking to *her*? I need to put an end to that. Whatever that was. I wouldn't let anything or *anyone* come between our future.

I shoved off my seat and continued to watch them as they continued their conversation. He was speaking emphatically, as if distressed about something. She kept nodding and then shook her head. Were they dating? It couldn't be.

I suppose she was pretty enough in a classic-beauty kind of way, but the whole goth look was a bit much if you asked me.

Now he was gesturing with both hands in the air, clasping them together as if begging her. Begging her for what? A date? You've got to be kidding me. Fury shot through my body. He didn't need to beg anyone to go out with him. Who did she think she was?

The petite, dark-haired girl shook her head and practically stormed off. What the heck? I'd been following him for weeks and I hadn't discovered any evidence inside his apartment that a woman had been around. At least not from what I could see through his bedroom window.

But just in case, I'd look into her. Maybe follow her, find out who she was and what business she had with *my man*. There was something curious and familiar about her, but I couldn't put my finger on it.

Was she an old girlfriend he was trying to get back together with? She obviously wasn't into it. If that was the case, that bitch didn't know what she'd had. *Whatever*. I'd make sure she stayed away and kept away. If she didn't, I'd send her the message loud and clear. He is mine. Well, maybe not mine, yet, but he would be and if goth girl knew what was good for her, she'd stay away from *my man*.

2

SELENA

I RUSHED OUT OF THE LECTURE HALL, PULLING AT MY collar, struggling for air as I pushed open the heavy wooden door and escaped out into the cool fall air. The breeze hit me in the face, cooling my skin while I took deep breaths in and out until my heartbeat steadied. I glanced around before heading toward the parking lot. I hurried my steps to avoid any attempted follow-up from Dillon.

I unzipped the pocket on the front of my backpack and pulled out my keys. I inserted the key into the lock of my car door and paused. A flurry of shame washed over me. Would I ever be normal? Could I ever move on? It had been a year and a half. Eighteen months. It felt like it was a lifetime ago, yet other times it seemed like only a moment had passed. The moment I knew in my guts that Brendon had been killed. Because of me. It was my fault he would never be a lawyer or a politician fighting for the rights of others. Never a father or a husband. He was nothing but a decaying body lying in a box in the ground. My heart hurt now as much as it had the day of his funeral.

Nobody had blamed me for his death, except for myself and maybe, secretly, his parents. The police department's official statement was that they suspected the heinous crime was committed by a network of human traffickers operating in the San Francisco Bay Area. Any association between Brendon's murder and my investigation into the traffickers was shielded from the press, thanks to my stepmother, Martina, and her connections at the police department.

It worked for a while until a few ruthless members of the press had discovered that I, Brendon's girlfriend, was not only a local college student but a junior private investigator linked to the discovery of the trafficking ring. Speculation into the connection went viral. It wasn't pretty. I'd shut down the few social media accounts I had and distanced myself from family and friends to keep them out of harm's way.

I never would have suspected a year and a half ago, when I had received my first official investigative assignment to look into the disappearance of a seven-year-old girl named Emily, that it would lead me into the dark world of human trafficking. I hadn't even known that trafficking was a thing in the Bay Area and the rest of the United States. I had discovered the ugly reality and wanted to not only save the girl but to take down the trafficking ring. I hadn't realized that while I was investigating them, they were investigating me. A few days before Brendon's death, the traffickers had warned me they would hurt Brendon if I didn't drop the case, but my drive to find Emily and my naivete about the seriousness of the threat resulted in the traffickers making good on their promise. It was my fault and I *would* find the people responsible for his death.

I don't know what it was about Dillon and his pleading for my help that triggered these memories. Maybe it was because Dillon reminded me of Brendon. His boyish charm. His drive. The crooked smile. I wanted to help him, but I couldn't. I was too close to my goals to be derailed now.

And Martina had been crystal clear. If I wanted her recommendation and sign-off for the required hours to obtain my private investigator's license, I couldn't take on any cases. She'd barely let me stay on at Drakos Monroe Security & Investigations, and even then I was only allowed to review records. Martina said I was lucky to do that after I'd violated about a hundred rules and a few laws during the trafficking case. The job was now painfully dull and a tremendous blow to my ego. If I didn't want my license or need access to the computer systems at the firm in order to covertly investigate the human trafficking ring and track down Brendon's killers, I would have quit the day he died.

Another stipulation from Martina, who was not only my boss but my stepmother, was that besides avoiding investigations, sanctioned or otherwise, I had to graduate from college first. I'm not sure she had expected that I would take a full class load over the last two summers and would graduate a semester early. But I was. I was so close. Three months. In three months, I would be a graduate of San Francisco University with a degree in criminal justice and a minor in business. I would apply for my private investigator's license and then... stay at Drakos Monroe Security & Investigations or would I branch out on my own or would I go into law enforcement? *Ugh.* I wasn't sure what I'd be doing after December, but I knew that I couldn't wait any longer to start the rest of my life. I no longer wanted to live under Martina's thumb or to be confined to the classroom. I wanted to take action. I would find who killed Brendon and bring them to justice. The question was, would I do it with a badge or a PI license?

A tap on my shoulder broke my concentration, causing my body to react using my self-defense training. I swung around ready and positioned my body into a fighting stance. The shock in Dillon's eyes caused me to stand down. The fact he'd gotten that close to me without detection was a clear sign my head wasn't on straight. I need to get it together. *Selena, get it together, like now.*

He shook his head. "I'm so sorry, I didn't intend to startle you."

"What do you want? I told you, I can't help you."

Dillon had read online about the trafficking case and knew I had worked as a private investigator, which was why he'd asked for my help with his alleged stalker. If you asked me, it sounded more like there was a girl who had a crush on him than the work of a sinister stalker. Notes left on his car. Notes slipped under his front door. Texts from an unknown number. What was the big deal? Was there something he was leaving out? His fear made little sense to me. But then again, I hadn't asked what the notes or texts said.

"I know that's what you said, but you're my only hope. I can't afford to pay an investigation firm. I don't have a lot of money, but maybe there is something I could do for you in exchange? I can cook. I could bring you meals or something else. Take class notes for you? Just name it. Please, this person is really scaring me."

I studied his face. He seemed honestly scared of whoever had been leaving him notes and sending texts. What did they say? I shook out the thoughts. I couldn't get involved.

"Look, I was barely allowed to keep working at my stepmother's investigation firm, and the only way she would let me stay on was if I swore to stay clear of any active investigations. Not to mention, I have a full load this semester. I can refer you to another firm or even to somebody else at my stepmother's firm. I'm sorry, but like I said before, I can't help you."

Why couldn't he leave me alone? I didn't know how else to explain it to him. *Get a clue, buddy.*

He lowered his head, sinking into himself.

Something stirred inside me. Pity? Guilt? *Push it down, girl.*

He glanced up at me. "Okay. I'm sorry to have bothered you. Take care."

I watched as he slinked off, defeated. I shook my head and then opened my car door and sunk into my seat, resting my head on the steering wheel, thinking about Dillon. I prayed to the Universe that his 'stalker' was just a jilted ex or a shy co-ed with a crush and not a genuine threat. If that were the case, why did I feel this way? Why was my gut screaming at me to help him? I squeezed my eyes shut. *Selena, you can do this. In three months you can help anyone you want. Dillon will be fine. You will be fine.* I took a deep breath before lifting my head and buckling my seat belt. As I drove out of the lot, I thought, *at least I'll have something new to discuss with my therapist this week.*

3

DILLON

I slunk back to my car. Selena must think I'm a total loser who can't even handle a secret admirer. It wasn't true, but maybe I was overreacting — Selena thought I was. Maybe I should have come clean with her about my suspicions of who might be behind the messages? At first I thought it might be Jenna. What a train wreck that relationship ended up being. I had no idea she was crazy until I'd broken up with her. We'd only dated a few months. It had been fun for a while but she turned clingy, and I just wasn't that into her. So I broke up with her. To say she didn't take it well was an understatement. She screamed and cried, insisting I was a cheater and that I'd pay for what I'd done to her. I didn't even know how to respond to her accusations. I hadn't cheated on her or mistreated her. I didn't understand her extreme reaction and hadn't been prepared for it.

The morning after the breakup, I discovered that all the tires on my car were flat. I'd confronted her, and she denied doing it, but the gleam in her eyes and snarky laughter, saying I deserved it, told me everything I needed to know. I tried to stay clear of her, but she started texting me insults almost daily and that was before she'd started rumors around school that I was into little boys. I had been so angry, I didn't know what to do. I confronted her again, and all she did was laugh in my face. Shortly after, she found a new boyfriend, another sucker, and she'd left me alone. That was a year ago.

My first thought when the notes started appearing, was that maybe Jenna had broken up with her new boyfriend and was restarting her plan to ruin me. I'm still not convinced it's not Jenna, but there are things that make me question her involvement. For starters, the person refers to herself in texts, emails, and hand-written notes as KT. Jenna had no issue using her actual identity before, but then again she could have convinced one of her friends to do the dirty work for her. But the other odd thing was the content of the messages. "You look great in blue." And "The new haircut looks amazing." It makes me believe the person is following me. Watching me. It was unnerving. On more than one occasion, I could feel the hairs on the back of my neck stand up when I sensed I was being watched. That wasn't normal. Or maybe I just didn't understand women.

I haven't been able to shake the feeling of being stalked, and now the messages were coming more frequently. I didn't like it and wanted it to stop. What if this person wasn't even a female? Maybe it's some deranged psychopath who messed with people for the fun of it. I didn't know if this was a harmless crush, revenge from Jenna, or a real threat. One thing I did know — whoever this is has all my contact information and knows where I live. Maybe I should block my phone number, change my email and move on. Maybe that was the smart thing to do. If it worked, and the person left me alone, all's well that ends well. I supposed it was worth a shot.

I hesitated as I approached the steps up to my apartment door, half expecting to find another note or worse. It was clear. Nothing on the front step. I inserted the key into the lock, but when the key turned easily, I realized it was unlocked. My breath seized. Why was the door unlocked? I stepped inside, entering slowly. I glanced to the right into the kitchen and spotted a bouquet of red roses wrapped in cellophane. Strange. Ryan wasn't the romantic or serious type in any of his relationships. I couldn't imagine whom he may have bought them for. Footsteps to the left. I turned my head to look, heart pounding. I let out a sigh. Ryan had forgotten to lock the door again. We had talked about this *many* times.

He ruffled the hairs on the back of his head. "Hey bro."

I let out an audible sigh. "You left the front door unlocked again."

"Sorry bro, but uh, you got a present. Must be from that whacky girl of yours," he chuckled.

At least somebody was amused by all of this. We both walked over to the breakfast counter. "Did these get delivered?"

"No, bro. They were on the doorstep. There's a note."

On the doorstep. She was here, again. "When did you get home?"

"I don't know, like five-ten minutes ago. They were just sitting there in front of the door. It's your lucky day, bro."

Lucky? That wasn't how I felt. "What does the note say?" I was afraid to look. I wish it would all just stop.

"I didn't check. I didn't want to be all up in your biz with this chick."

Ryan and I had been roommates for a little over a month. He was a freshman and still acted like the teenager he was. All chicks and dudes and bro. He wasn't a terrible roommate, but he got on my nerves. *Often.* He wasn't quite a grown-up yet.

I stepped closer and picked up the white envelope with my name written on it in block letters. I opened the flap and pulled out a white card and flipped it open. I cocked my head as I read it to myself.

SHE ISN'T RIGHT FOR YOU.
YOU AND I WERE MEANT TO BE TOGETHER.
TRUST ME. PLEASE STAY AWAY FROM HER.
WE'LL BE TOGETHER SOON.
LOVE ALWAYS,
KT

My mind went into overdrive, trying to understand what it meant. Who was the 'she' that KT was referring to?

"What does it say?"

I read the note aloud to Ryan.

"Who is she talking about?"

She's not right for you? I shook my head. "I don't know. Maybe..." A sinking feeling came over me. Selena. Had KT been watching me and had seen me talking to Selena? That was just today - KT was at my apartment - minutes before I'd arrived. "I don't know. She might be referring to Selena."

"Who's Selena?"

"She's in one of my classes. She works for a private investigation firm. I asked her for help to figure out who's been sending me all these notes. I talked to her today - not more than thirty minutes ago."

"Wow. Bro. That's nuts. Wait, is this Selena hot?"

Was she? I would describe her as beautiful as opposed to hot, but she's more than that. She was intense and interesting and different. Intimidating. "She's attractive."

Ryan's eyes were wide. "Wait. Bro. A PI? Hot? Dude, is she that chick I've heard about who's boyfriend got whacked like a few years back? I'd stay clear of her. You might end up like the last guy." He put his pointer finger to his neck and swept it across.

I rolled my eyes at Ryan. He was such a juvenile.

"Bro. I'm teasing. But is it her, for reals?"

"It's her." That's how I knew to ask her for help. The story had been all over social media my junior year. It was no wonder that Selena mostly kept to herself. But it wasn't like Selena had killed her boyfriend. She didn't seem like she could hurt anybody — well unless someone messed with her. She definitely had a hardness to her.

"Is she going to help?"

"She said no."

"Bummer." Ryan's eyes studied the tiny screen as he scrolled. "I hate to add to the bad news, but you need to check Facebook."

"What? Why?"

"It's what I came out to tell you. I think you need to see it for yourself."

I pulled out my iPhone from my back pocket. I opened up the Facebook app and scrolled through my notifications. My mouth dropped open. KTSpencer 0724 and I were 'in a relationship.'

Spencer was my last name.

My birthday was July 24.

The situation was getting too weird, and it didn't feel like Jenna. It wasn't right. It wasn't normal. It was abnormal — like the kind of abnormal I'd learned about in my psychology courses. My major was to understand the human mind, but I couldn't figure out KT's and that scared the hell out of me.

Sure I could block KT's number, change my email, and delete all my social media accounts and then what, go into hiding?

Ryan strolled over and patted me on the shoulder. "Congrats on the new relationship."

I tightened my jaw.

"Dude, chill. I was joking. Maybe you should try to meet up

with her. Ask her out, then you'll know who it is. Who knows, maybe she's hot. The crazy ones always are."

Although Ryan was stupid and it was a stupid thing to say, it wasn't like I hadn't asked KT her actual identity. But KT insisted that when it was the right time, we'd be together. Whatever that meant. I could try to push for a meeting and put an end to this secret identity crap. But something about her seemed unhinged, dangerous even. Who changes their relationship status on Facebook with somebody they've never even spoken to in person?

Maybe these latest actions, the flowers and note about Selena, would be enough for Selena to take me seriously and help me figure out KT's true identity and her motive.

It really was strange. This wasn't just a secret admirer gone too far. She watched me. Visited my apartment. Announced on social media that we were in a relationship.

Selena had been clear that she wasn't able to take on any active investigations, but maybe she would meet with me and at least help me figure out how I could investigate on my own. Surely that wouldn't violate her stepmother's rules. I needed Selena's help. I hoped that I could convince her this time. If Selena wouldn't help me, I don't know what I would do. Hide?

4

SELENA

I RAN THROUGH MY LIST OF TO-DO ITEMS IN MY MIND AS I strolled through the corridor. After target practice and dinner with Dee, I still had homework, and I'd like to take a trip to the office to catch up on some secret investigating, but it might be too late at night to look legit. I needed to come up with a reason to be there after hours. I would have to search through my work notes to see if there was something I could use as a cover.

I stepped into the crosswalk toward the parking lot when I heard a now-familiar voice call out my name. "Selena."

This guy just didn't seem to take a hint or an explicit 'no' for that matter. I pivoted and watched as he jogged toward me. By the time he stopped, he was out of breath. He must have been following me for a while. I was too lost in my own thoughts to notice. That wasn't good news for me. I needed to be more alert. Where had all my training gone? Without being on 'active duty' I suppose I'd slacked off a little. I hated being a desk jockey. A file reviewer. I'd much rather be out on the streets investigating. Getting justice. I put on my best friendly-but-annoyed look. I think I pulled it off. "Dillon, what's up?"

"Thanks for stopping. I..."

I was about to interrupt him when he raised his hand. "Please, please. I know you told me you couldn't help me, but if you can give me five minutes to explain."

I studied him. His eyes were pleading and desperate. Under different circumstances, he'd be pretty cute. Friendly. Warm. Not the current mess that stood before me. I glanced at the screen on my phone in my hand and then back up at him. "Five minutes. I have to be somewhere, so really only five." I didn't have to be rude, he was a classmate and clearly in distress. Giving him five minutes wouldn't hurt anything, right?

"Thanks. I'll be quick. I understand you can't help investigate, but things have gotten really out of hand and it's freaking me out. I don't want to get you into trouble at your job or with your stepmother, so I was thinking maybe you could give me some tips on how to investigate on my own? How to make it stop."

Out of hand? "What do you mean out of hand?" *Why was I asking? Selena, no. Girl, walk away.*

He shook his head in anguish. "When I got home after school yesterday, you know, after we spoke in the parking lot, there were flowers and a note waiting for me. My roommate said he found them when he'd arrived a few minutes earlier. The note referred to 'she'll never make you happy like I can'. It took me a minute to figure out who KT could have been referring to, but then I realized maybe it was you she was talking about. If that's true, she must have followed me and saw us together and assumed it was some kind of romantic connection."

He paused and looked like he was waiting for my reaction. I mean, I certainly didn't like the idea of someone watching me. *Still, walk away. Like now.*

He continued, "That's not even everything. She has this fictional Facebook profile and she just posted that she's in a relationship with me. I don't even know this person. She's watching me. She's calling me. She's texting me. She knows where I live."

I listened as he continued to give me the bizarre details. A stalker - a genuine stalker was never good. At first, I had thought maybe he was being hypersensitive and that this was an ex-girl-friend seeking revenge. Now I understood why he was so upset about this, it wasn't normal. Even so, something didn't seem quite right, like he was holding something back. "So, you're telling me everything that this 'KT' has done. And you're sure it's not an ex-girlfriend or somebody you know?"

He closed his eyes and huffed.

Interesting.

When he opened his eyes again, he looked at me. "Okay, so I don't know that for sure. And to be honest, at first I suspected it was an ex, someone I dated last year. Jenna didn't take the breakup well. She let the air out of my tires. She spread rumors about me, I'm surprised you hadn't heard, she said I was a pedophile which I am not, by the way. She said it just to hurt me. But when she found a new guy, her lashing out stopped. Eventually the rumors faded and my life was peaceful and normal. I thought it was all behind me and that my senior year would be a good one, but then this all started up and I suspected Jenna, but it was more bizarre than anything Jenna had ever done. Jenna never concealed her identity and she didn't follow me, that I know of. This seems different. Off."

I contemplated his confession. The ex had moved on and maybe she and the new boyfriend broke up and she sought revenge on Dillon again. Maybe she was bored or maybe had enlisted a friend to help her. Ugh. I needed to stop thinking about this case. Not a case. Don't call it a case. This potential investigation, that I will not be involved in, was interesting. More interesting than reviewing phone records and looking for patterns. That was my job now. For now. *Three months, Selena, you can and will make it.* Maybe I could give him a few tips - maybe. I glanced at my phone again. "Look, I really gotta go. It sounds bizarre. I'll give you that. I just..."

He clasped his hands together. "I'm begging you. Please, just think about it. Maybe you could share some tips on how I can figure out who this is. Like, do you know how to find out someone's IP address? And how to track KT's location? You could be a teacher, not an investigator. I can't pay a lot, but I have a little. Please, at least say you'll think about it."

"I have to go, but I'll think about it." *Selena, what are you doing? Say no!*

A grin spread across his face and his eyes lit up. "Thank you so much, Selena. Thank you."

"I haven't agreed to anything yet."

"I appreciate that you're even considering helping me. If you decide you can help, just call or text me anytime." He handed me his phone, and I begrudgingly entered my contact information into it and he did the same with mine. I really needed to learn how to say no. *For reals.*

I STOOD WITH MY ARMS OUTSTRETCHED AND A POWERFUL weapon in my hand. I stared through my shooting glasses at the faceless target in front of me. On paper he was faceless but in my mind he had a face. He was every one of the predators at the DKA house. He was Ocampo. He was the trafficker who took Brendon from me and the rest of the world. He was my enemy, and I was going to take him down.

A tap on my shoulder caused me to lower my weapon and turn my head. I mouthed, 'one more', before returning to my target.

Bam. Bam. Head. Chest. Done and done. There's something quite meditative about shooting a gun and in your mind imagining the destruction of your enemy and making the world a safer place. One day it would be for real.

After I removed my safety gear, I packed up my gun, which had been a 21st birthday present from Dad and Martina. The night of my 21st, instead of getting blasted on booze and God knows what else, Martina took Dee and I to the firing range and I shot a gun for the very first time. It had been a life-altering moment.

The power I held in my hands made it clear to me that not only was owning a gun important but that I also needed to become highly skilled in shooting. I needed my PI license and a concealed carry permit, so I'd never be vulnerable again.

I wondered if knowing that one day, and hopefully one day soon, I'd be able to carry a lethal weapon for protection, had caused me to slack off on my hand-to-hand combat training. My healthy diet. Not that I had gone completely bananas, I still ran three days a week but had added ice cream and the occasional margarita with Dee to my menu. Considering Dillon had snuck up on me and now it appeared I had someone following me without my knowledge, I should really start hitting the gym again. As it was, my pants were a bit more snug than was comfortable.

Ok, fine.

I admit I'd become complacent, but sitting at a desk pushing papers and studying numbers wasn't doing me any favors. Martina had warned me to keep up with my training, to prepare me for when I was active again. It had been a year and a half. *Sigh.* I suppose Martina was right *again*. It was so annoying sometimes.

I couldn't wait to get back out there fighting for the little guy.

I shut the door of my rented cubby, entered my passcode to

lock it and headed toward Dee, who was now chatting with the owner of the facility. I approached with a little pep in my step. "Hey Dee." I always felt better after a session at the shooting range.

"You ready to go?"

"Yep."

Dee said, "See you later, Marco."

I waved as I followed behind Dee. I told her, "I can drive if you want."

"Cool. Works for me."

On the road, heading toward our favorite dinner place, I asked Dee, "What's new?"

"I've been super busy."

She described her schedule. Dee was one seriously ambitious woman — not only was she double-majoring in chemistry and psychology with plans to become a psychiatrist, she was also a volunteer at the crisis center on campus. She had the lofty goal of dedicating her life to advocating for and helping other people - more specifically, survivors of sexual and physical trauma.

Her mission started after she was attacked during our first year of college, at the DKA fraternity house. As with most people who are survivors of such violence, it forever changed her life. Just thinking about the incident made my blood boil. Sure, I'd exposed the systemic violence that was happening at the fraternity, they'd lost their charter, and one man was arrested, but it still rattled me. I had a hard time letting go of the fact that some of the men involved hadn't been brought to justice. It was little solace that the fraternity was disbanded.

Dee had been more forgiving than me, and after some intense counseling she'd channeled her pain into making other's lives better. She had been a science major intending to go to medical school prior to the attack, but now she had shifted her focus to helping others heal mentally instead of physically. With her double major and volunteer work, there wasn't room for much else.

She hadn't dated anyone since her attack. I didn't blame her, as I was in the same camp a few years earlier for slightly different reasons. I'd also been attacked, but it was by my high school boyfriend, who not only forced himself on me but also tried to kill me. *Boys will be boys, am I right? Sigh.* Yes, he in fact turned out to be a murderer and I was lucky to have survived. If it wasn't for Martina, I wouldn't have. It was a crazy way to meet my future stepmother and reconnect with my former-addict dad, but it turned out to be perfect timing.

I had sworn off dating after that. It wasn't until I'd met Brendon and he'd worn me down, that I broke my rule. Brendon managed to change my view on everything about relationships. He showed me that men could be good and loving. Relationships could be healthy. And could also end suddenly in a life-shattering moment.

If I could've taken Brendon's place, I would have - in a heartbeat. Since that wasn't a possibility, I had focused all of my free time on the continued investigation into the traffickers, albeit secretly. But after my mistakes caused his death, I vowed I wouldn't let it happen again. I couldn't put my loved ones at risk, so I had kept my distance to keep them safe.

I stopped living with Dee, or anyone, and I kept family visits to a minimum. I limited most of my interaction with Martina to when I was at the offices of Drakos & Monroe, but even then I didn't seek her out. I had to make sure she wouldn't catch on to my secret investigation into Brendon's killers.

I had finally caved in to Dee's insistence that we should keep in touch. She suggested shooting practice and food dates and argued that since we both practiced regularly, there was no reason for us to not meet up and practice together. And get a bite to eat afterward. Dee was quite persuasive. I missed spending more time with her. She was the one who suggested I take on extra classes to graduate early. Dee was one smart cookie.

I tapped my fingers on the steering wheel, and Dee shifted her attention to me. "What's going on with you, Selena? If I didn't know better, I'd say you have something on your mind."

Did I have something on my mind? *Yes.* The world. My past. My present. Dillon. "I've been thinking a lot about things lately. Bad things. I think the memories were stirred up by one of my classmates who has been begging for my help." I told her all the details about Dillon's case - not a case - and explained that I was still determining whether I should help him investigate his stalker. I pulled into the parking lot at the Happy Fortune, a Chinese restaurant that we both loved. It wasn't a healthy choice, but it was a delicious one. I was halfway out of the car when I realized Dee hadn't moved. I stuck my leg back in and shut the door and turned to her. "What?"

Her face was long. "Selena, I think you should help him."

"Why?"

"From what you described, those aren't normal activities. Sorry if I sound like a brand-new psych major, but this stalker, KT, could have some kind of personality disorder or other serious mental health issue. This person who is watching him, and you, could be seriously disturbed and capable of hurting Dillon, you, or themselves. Or all of the above. I think you should help Dillon."

I contemplated what Dee had explained. Did this mean it wasn't Jenna, his ex? Unless Jenna had some sort of disorder or whatever Dee was going on about. "So, you really think we could be in danger?"

Dee sunk into her shoulders. "I mean, maybe, maybe not. It sounds like this person is escalating and may become more unhinged, which could lead them to do unpredictable and dangerous things. And now that you're in their sights, Selena, you could be in danger. I think even if you're not doing this for Dillon, you should do it for yourself. Martina would have to understand, you're not taking on a new investigation, you're just helping him and yourself without actually breaking her rules and jeopardizing your PI license."

I studied Dee's wide, aqua-blue eyes. Dee was right. I wasn't technically taking on an investigation. Helping Dillon wouldn't break the rules, so it was okay, and I probably didn't even *need* to tell Martina about it. After all, his life and my own could be in danger. I'd be foolish not to help, right?

5

TAYLOR

Through my sunglasses, I spotted her in the quad sitting at a table, book open, head down. It was a perfect opportunity to get to know his new friend. I casually strolled over to the table across from her. "Mind if I sit here?"

She glanced up at me with her chocolate-brown eyes and gave a friendly smile. "Sure." She returned her gaze back to her economics book.

I placed my backpack down on the bench and pulled out my own economics book and said, "You're in my econ class, right?"

She looked up without moving her head. "Maybe?"

I climbed over the bench and sat. "Professor Donna, nine a.m., Monday, Wednesday, and Friday."

She lifted a brow and sat up straight. "Yeah, that's my class. Not sure I've seen you in there before."

She seemed defensive for such a benign question. She must be a strange one. "I usually sit in the back. I'm not really a front-row-hand-raiser, you know?"

She mumbled. "Uh, huh?"

"I'm Taylor March." I stretched my hand across the table.

She set her pencil down on her book and shook my hand. "I'm Selena Bailey."

"Great to meet you. I like the tattoo on your wrist. What does it mean?"

She looked at her wrist as if she didn't know it was there. She was definitely a strange one - or at the very least, not a friendly person. I couldn't possibly be the first person to ask about her tattoo. "It's a Celtic symbol."

"Oh cool, are you Irish?"

"No."

Okay. She is definitely a strange one. "Awesome weather we're having, isn't it? I decided to study outside today to absorb the rays since we probably won't have many more sunny days this year. Gray skies and fog will arrive any minute, with no more sunshine until the spring."

Selena nodded, and her body seemed to relax. "I agree, it's nice, that's why I came out here to study too."

Maybe I'd finally broken through her wall. "Are you from around here?"

"East Bay."

"Seriously? Where about? I'm from Walnut Creek."

She hesitated. "All around, mostly Grapton Hill."

"We're practically neighbors. Are you a freshman?"

Selena picked up her pencil. "No, this is my last semester. I'm graduating in December."

"Really? I didn't know you could graduate anytime other than spring, but I'm not an expert. I'm a freshman. This is my first semester of college, ever."

She nodded as if that explained everything. I may be young, but I wasn't too young to know what I wanted.

"Yep, it's possible. This is my fourth year, but I took extra classes so I could graduate early. It keeps me pretty busy."

Okay, okay. I know you're hinting for me to leave you alone, but sorry, I need info. "Wow, you must be so smart. Are you majoring in economics?"

She let out a breath. "No, my major is criminal justice with a business minor."

"Cool. I'm majoring in business."

She barely nodded. "Well, it was nice meeting you, I should probably get back to studying."

I was losing her. "Oh yeah, of course. So sorry to bother you, but I'm curious. I thought I saw you with Dillon Spencer after class, is he your boyfriend?"

She cocked her head. "No, he's not my boyfriend."

"No? He seems nice? And he's cute, right?"

She hesitated. "He seems nice, I guess, but I'm not interested."

"Do you have a boyfriend? Is that why you can't date him?"

She seemed to tense back up.

"Oh, sorry, I didn't mean to assume. Maybe you have a girl-friend?" *That must be why she turned Dillon down. It was the only logical reason.*

"No, it's not that, I just don't date anyone."

"Bad experience?"

She snorted. "To put it mildly, I'm sorry I don't mean to be rude, but I really need to finish my homework."

I glanced over at her paper and saw that she'd been working on our economic's homework and was halfway done with it. From what I could tell, she had got them all right. So what I'd learned so far was that she was smart, she was graduating early, and she didn't date. Maybe she wasn't the threat I thought she was, but for good measure I'd look into her further. "I'm so sorry. I'll leave you to it. It was nice meeting you."

She waved her hand and said, "no problem," before returning her focus to her homework. *Yes, Selena Bailey, I must find out more about you.*

After studying for an hour across from her, I skipped back to my dorm room high on sunshine and knowing that Dillon wasn't dating Selena. It didn't mean I was completely out of the woods yet. After all, he kept going after her for something, begging her for a date or something else?

I opened the door to my suite and studied the living room. Dirty dishes covered the dining table, and the sofa had a sweatshirt and books strewn about. My roommate was such a slob, but thankfully she wasn't home much. I loved the idea of living alone. Sometimes I wished she would go home or trip and fall off a balcony just so I'd have the place to myself. Not that Mandy was a bad person, she was actually nice to me, but I'd love to have my own space. I thrived on the freedom college enabled. I had goals, and I was going to achieve them. Nobody would get in my way.

I shut the door behind me and put my backpack on the floor by the sofa. My cell phone buzzed in my hand. "Hey, what's up?"

"I just wanted to ask you if you're going to be bringing your new boyfriend home at Thanksgiving?"

"It's a little early for Thanksgiving, don't you think?"

Why was she all over me? It wasn't even October. Why was she planning a holiday that was two months away? Of course, I will probably bring Dillon with me.

"Don't take that tone with me, Taylor."

My body filled with fury. "I'll take whatever tone I want. I am an adult and you keep pestering me and bothering me. Why can't you let me live my life! If you keep at it, you'll be lucky if I come home for Thanksgiving." I ended the call and slammed the phone on the couch. I was so sick of people trying to control my life. I huffed and puffed as I stomped around my dorm room. I wanted to break something. Ugh. How was it that my stupid mother could still elicit these kinds of feelings inside of me? I wanted to scream and cry. Why couldn't she just let me live my life? I couldn't be controlled. I am my own person. They couldn't live my life for me. I was more than capable of pursuing my dreams and achieving all I set my mind to. I will get what I want and when I want it - *any means necessary*.

6

SELENA

I pulled my jacket closed as I approached the small café in North Beach where I was meeting Dillon. There was a line of twenty patrons outside the door. It must be a popular place. Hopefully, he'd thought ahead and we wouldn't be waiting out in the cold. I turned to the left and peered through the glass doors to see inside. I spotted Dillon sitting at a small table for two. I opened the door, and the breeze ruffled the napkins at a nearby table. I shut it behind me and headed towards Dillon. He looked up and waved. I put my backpack on the back of the chair and sat down in front of him. "Hi."

"Hey. I didn't know what you liked to drink, so I ordered two double espressos. Is that okay? I can always get you something else. I had to order to get a table." He said sheepishly.

I glanced down at the tiny cup and saucer with a miniature biscotti on the side. I inhaled the strong coffee aroma. It was heavenly. I glanced around the small café that contained only fifteen small tables for two. I focused my attention back on Dillon, his light-blue eyes were full of hope. I gave him a reassuring smile. "It's perfect, thank you." I didn't normally drink espresso, but anything with caffeine was fine with me.

He fidgeted, crinkling his napkin with his fingers. "Did you find the café okay?"

"It was no problem, I used to eat down here all the time." North Beach was a predominantly Italian part of San Francisco filled with restaurants serving great pasta, coffee, and gelato. It had been a while since I'd visited. The area always reminded me of Brendon since our first date was at a restaurant just around the corner. A dull pain sat in my chest.

Dillon nodded. "Great to hear it."

"Do you come down here a lot?" I wasn't usually a fan of small talk, but if we were going to work together, I should know more about him.

"Occasionally. This café is my favorite. The food is amazing, and the coffee is even better. I'm a bit of a coffee buff and this place has the best coffee in the entire city - probably California. It's pretty amazing, try it."

I picked up the tiny white cup and sipped. It was rich and velvety. Not what I was expecting. "It's good."

He grinned, showing off his dimples. "Glad you like it."

Suddenly it was feeling like a first date, although that wasn't the purpose. Despite knowing that, it filled my stomach with butterflies that wouldn't stop flittering around. They had arrived without my consent. *Unacceptable.* I took another sip, trying to hide my angst. I wasn't sure what it was about Dillon that had me flustered. I hadn't expected that. I swatted the butterflies and then cleared my head. "Anything new happen with KT since we spoke yesterday?" It was my rather abrupt attempt to bring the situation back to a non-date-like atmosphere. Down to business. I needed to keep it strictly business.

"No, nothing out of the ordinary. She texts me every day, but hasn't posted anything new on Facebook today. I have no idea how to find out who she is and make it all stop. Thank you again for agreeing to meet with me and for helping me. I appreciate it more than you know."

"Sure. Based on our previous conversations, you're getting text messages, email messages, and someone is connecting with you on Facebook and pretending to be in a relationship with you. She knows where you live, where you go to school and where you work. My guess is she's a student at the school. I say this because she was able to watch and follow you, going from class to your car, watch us in the parking lot and then afterward, go to your apartment and leave flowers and a note. Is that everything?"

He nodded. "Yeah, that's everything."

"Well, if I were investigating, which I'm not. The first thing I would do is try to determine the IP addresses used for email and Facebook. Second, I would look at the phone number from the text messages and try to find out, based on phone records, who the phone number belongs to."

"Do IP addresses and phone records always say who it belongs to?"

"No, not necessarily. If the IP address is registered to a specific user, we'll get the identity based on internet provider. On the flip side, if KT used a public library, the IP address won't give us her identity, but we may get the address of the computer used, and we could go from there. Her phone records may identify the user if it's registered, but it's easy enough to get a burner phone. All you'd have to do is walk into any drugstore and buy a phone for twenty bucks. They're not traceable, so if that is what KT used, it'll be a dead end."

"What happens if I can't get a name or address?"

Then we're working with somebody who may have done this before and they'll be hard to find. Not good news. "We can address that when, or if, we get there, but what I would typically do, which I will not do because I'm not investigating this case, is follow you around and see if I could spot somebody watching you, but since you're doing this yourself, you must be hyper-vigilant and always be checking your surroundings and gaining awareness of those near and around you. You need to be on the lookout for anyone who keeps popping into your line of sight. Can you think of anybody you keep running into?"

"No, I don't think so. But I'll start looking, that's for sure."

I watched his long fingers pick up the coffee cup by the tiny handle. I shook the non-business thoughts from my mind. Keep focused. What was it about this guy?

He set the cup down. "Okay, so how do I find the IP address and get phone records? Is it something I can do over the internet?"

"Yeah, there are services on the internet, they do the search for a fee. That's where you should start."

"I'll do that. And then you and I can meet again to talk about what I find?"

I studied his face. It was a pleasant face, but I needed to keep my head clear and my eye on the prize. I should probably keep my distance. Official business only. "Sure, we can do that." I finished my espresso and then bit into the biscotti. Something I would not have done a year and a half ago, but now I eat biscotti, cookies, and waffles. Not that one little biscotti would derail my fitness. Dee and I had a date at her gym this weekend. This Saturday, I'd start my journey back to peak fitness. I was a little nervous and a lot excited to get closer to being my old self - or maybe even a better, tougher self.

"Thank you for the espresso, but I should really be going."

"Do you have to? You drove all the way out, I was thinking maybe we could grab a bite to eat. They have great sandwiches, pastas, pizzas, and quiches."

I watched him as he continued to rattle off practically the entire menu in the café. He was a nice guy. A good guy. A guy that didn't deserve to be anywhere near me when danger inevitably struck. Then again, I was already here. My stomach growled. I suppose that was my answer. "Oh, sure, I could eat."

My suspicious nature overcame me. Had he made up this entire story just to get to me to go out with him? Was he the psycho? Was I stupid for just taking his word for it? Could he be working with the traffickers? Was I helping a future deranged psychopath stalker? It was far-fetched, but I really needed to get back on my game. Anything was possible.

Dillon waved over a member of the waitstaff. She promptly hurried over, notepad in hand. We gave our order, and she quickly shuffled away.

"So what do you have planned for the rest of the day?" Dillon asked.

"Homework. You?"

"Oh, you know, homework, get IP addresses, phone records, and try not to get killed by a deranged stalker." He laughed nervously, clearly uneasy about the situation. My instinct told me he wasn't the psycho. Perhaps that's why I hadn't asked him for evidence and I wasn't actually losing my touch?

We made polite chit-chat while waiting for our food. It was very date-like, but it wasn't uncomfortable because he was charming. If I hadn't sworn off dating, I'd be happy to be here. It was nice. It felt normal. "So what plans do you have for after graduation?"

"I'm majoring in psychology with a minor in business, but I plan to go to law school. I want to work in entertainment."

"What a coincidence, I'm also minoring in business, but majoring in criminal justice. I can't wait to graduate in December."

"What do you plan to do after graduation?"

Well, now there's the million-dollar question. "I always thought I'd either go into law enforcement or private investigations. I'm leaning towards private investigations. So, I'll get my PI license and maybe start my own firm." I chuckled. "And when I say firm, I mean a tiny office in a strip mall somewhere, where I'll have to hustle to get clients to make a living. I really like the idea of owning my own business and becoming my own boss." I was more than a little tired of taking orders from Martina and the rules at Drakos Monroe Security & Investigations.

"Wow. That's exciting. How did you get into investigations?"

"That's a long story, but the short of it is, my stepmother introduced me to it."

For the rest of the afternoon, we ate amazing pizza and talked about the future and the past. I, of course, omitted the nitty-gritty details and provided a candy-coated version of my history. I didn't need to frighten him; KT scared him enough. And if you examined my past too closely, it's pretty obvious that I've left a wake of dead bodies. I couldn't let Dillon become one of them.

Dillon had big plans. He wanted to be an entertainment lawyer representing talent to ensure artists weren't taken advantage of. He was bright and cute and cared about people, and I was actually enjoying myself with a man for the first time in a long time. Guilt and shame filled me. They say time heals all wounds. I don't know if that's true. I was still heartbroken over the loss of Brendon, but somehow Dillon was seeping inside of that same broken heart. Maybe we could be friends - from a distance.

When the check came, I offered to pay. It was best to appear to be nothing but business, but of course he insisted on paying. I reluctantly agreed, but he'd insisted it was his way of saying thanks.

I stood up and was about to grab my backpack when my phone buzzed in the front pocket. I pulled it out and looked at the screen — my body froze. I glanced up at Dillon who was standing there patiently waiting for me to walk out of the restaurant with him. "I just got a message from someone claiming to be KT."

His smile faded.

Now, this was personal.

7

DILLON

I held my breath as the colorful little wheel turned and turned. Damn it. I needed answers. I let out the breath that I'd been holding. Damn. The IP address traced back to multiple public locations on campus. It was my last hope since the phone number search turned up nada. Not registered. What was I going to do now? Call Selena? She hadn't told me what we'd do if none of the direct paths to the identity of KT panned out.

It appeared that there wasn't a simple way to know who was behind the Facebook account or the phone number KT was using to get to me. I couldn't for the life of me figure out what I did to deserve this. Why would anyone go through this much trouble to bother me? I have always tried to be a good person. I mean, I try. I work. I go to school. I call my mother every week.

For me, why was the biggest question, after the identification of KT. Based on the last three years of taking psychology classes, the whole situation made my gut churn. This person was not of sound mind. That same gut says it wasn't Jenna. I dated Jenna. I knew her. She was emotional and young, but not mentally ill. Was she? I hadn't thought she'd retaliate after our breakup, so maybe I didn't know her as well as I'd thought.

What could I do? Would Selena break her rules and help me further? She'd said the next step typically would be to follow me to see if anybody was watching me, but she couldn't help me. I didn't want to get her into trouble at her job or jeopardize the PI license she wanted so badly. I didn't want Selena hurt because of all this. No, I had to be extra vigilant and pay attention to everyone around me. How could I possibly do that all the time? Should I reach out to Jenna to eliminate her as a suspect? Assuming she'd take my call. If she was KT, she probably would. It makes me sick to think that this KT may be dangerous. What if she went after Selena? Maybe I should drop the whole thing.

I shut the lid of my laptop and pulled out my phone to call Selena to let her know what I'd found, or rather hadn't found. My heart raced thinking about her. The sound of her voice and the memory of how her hair smells. Fruity. There was something about Selena I couldn't shake. Even with my nerves on overdrive, I couldn't help being drawn to her. Her flawless olive skin and curves in all the right places. Gorgeous. I shook my head.

I could fantasize all I wanted, but I knew I couldn't cross that line, not with her, it wouldn't be right. Maybe it would better if I texted her instead of hearing or seeing her. When I was with her, I didn't want to leave her presence. I wanted to know everything about Selena Bailey. She'd told me about her career ambitions and I'd read about her past. She was definitely the most intriguing woman I had ever known. Damn it. I need to make this KT person exit my life.

This situation was making me nuts. I'd text her.

I tapped out a message.

Hi Selena. IP addresses all public places. No matches on the phone number either. Any suggestions on what to do next? Thank you. Dillon.

I watched as the dots bounced up and down. She was up, and she was replying right away. I felt the tingling inside. I read the message.

That sucks. Keep an eye out. Be aware of your surroundings and who is around you. Let's talk more. Will you be at school tomorrow?

A smile crept up my face. I had planned on being at school, but even if I hadn't, I would've made a special trip.

I'll be there. You want to meet up after class?

I waited for her response.

Grab breakfast and talk about the case?

I needed to be cool. *Be cool, Dillon. Be cool.* I inserted a casual thumbs up, but then deleted it. Who was I kidding? I wasn't cool.

Sounds good. Have a good night.

My heart skipped as I saw the dancing dots once more.

Good night.

I sat back in my desk chair and looked around my apartment. The kitchen counters had stacks of dishes and empty cups. The living room had piles of clothes, takeout containers, and sporting equipment. My roommate was in his room, probably getting high. That was what it smelled like anyhow. A total mess. It was gross, but I would not clean up after my teenage roommate. I made a mental note to rent a one-bedroom when I went off to law school. I was done with roommates.

I opened up my laptop again to finish up the problem set for my finance class, but despite my best efforts, my mind drifted back to Selena. What would it be like to have her in my bed? To kiss those full lips, that body. I wanted all of her.

What if this stalker, this KT person, was the hardship I had to endure for finding the person I was supposed to spend my life with? What if Selena and I were meant to be together? Nothing easy was ever worth fighting for. What the heck was I thinking? Sure, she was hot. She was intriguing, but this wasn't some weird fairy tale; it wasn't a movie. I raked my fingers through my hair and shook my head. I really need to stop thinking like some lovesick puppy, I barely knew her. Plus, I had bigger fish to fry, like getting rid of a stalker and graduating from college. *Be cool, man. Be cool.*

8

SELENA

I SET MY CELL PHONE DOWN ON THE DESK WITH AN UNEASY feeling in my gut. Why hadn't I just told Dillon that I couldn't help and kept away from him? Something in me wanted to help him, and now this crazy person was texting me. Thankfully, it was just the one message from yesterday telling me to stay away from Dillon - nothing new today. But it definitely confirmed that KT knew my identity and had likely been watching me and Dillon talking in the parking lot. Maybe she even saw us together at the café. Maybe she was outside the restaurant watching us through the glass when she messaged me. *Creepy*.

There was a part of me wanted to tell Martina to see if maybe the firm could take the case pro bono, especially now that it may involve me. Maybe I should, but then I'd have to tell Martina everything, and I wasn't sure how she would take it. She may see it as a sign of defiance or worse, betrayal. We used to be close. Martina was like the mother I'd always wished I'd had. Even before my mom had been killed, she wasn't exactly winning parenting awards. It was a reverse child-and-parent scenario. I was the one with the steady job and took myself back-to-school shopping. Despite her flaws, I still missed her.

She had been fun and loving even, when she wasn't too drunk or with one of her loser boyfriends.

Martina was the darn near opposite. Reliable and calm. Tough and protective. Motherly. After she'd literally saved my life and I was all alone, Martina, my dad's fiance, reconnected me with my father, and the two of them took me in with open arms.

That was four years ago.

Since then, Martina has taken me under her wing, taught me how to defend myself, and introduced me to the world of private investigations. Martina and I had grown close over that time, up until I'd hidden away after getting my boyfriend killed while working on one of our cases. After Brendon, I shut everyone out, keeping them at arm's length to keep them safe. Not that Martina and I didn't meet regularly while I was at the office, but I tried to keep those meetings on topic and not get too personal. I had to. I still attended holiday gatherings and exchanged emails with my stepsister, Zoey.

Maybe wanting to help Dillon was more than just the desire to help him. I felt drawn toward him and I couldn't explain it. Maybe it was my loneliness. I missed having someone to talk to about little things. Simple things. Not about my past. Not about my failures. Somebody new who couldn't see all my warts and scars. A person I could go to a casual lunch with, not that our lunch had been casual - at first. We were there to discuss his potentially dangerous stalker, who then contacted me and for all I know was watching me as well. Why was life so complicated at what seemed like every turn? Why was there always a new challenge, seemingly worse than the one before? Why couldn't I settle for a happy, easy, calm life? What was it that was inside of me that drove me to face danger in the eye, staring it down until I claimed victory or justice? I supposed that was just the way I was wired.

Footsteps drew near, and I changed the display to show a legitimate work file. I glanced up. Martina had circles under her eyes, but wore a friendly smile. She must've had a long day. "You're here late." She said.

I was there late. I was hoping she'd already gone home. It was nearly 10 o'clock at night. Hopefully, the fact I was at the office late didn't prompt her to take away my keys to the office. "Yeah, just a few records I didn't get to yesterday, I wanted to look at them before the weekend."

"Which case?"

I wondered if she suspected I was coming in to work my secret investigation into Brendon's killers. If she did, she didn't say anything to me. We hadn't talked about Brendon in a long time. Not since the anniversary of his death, six months ago. She'd urged me to attend the vigil put on by his parent's church. I refused. I couldn't face them. I couldn't even bring myself to visit his grave. The guilt was too severe. I had to find his killers. I had to. My therapist said I should go to his grave to talk to him. To let him go. I didn't know if I could. Maybe once I found his killers, I could face him and be able to move on. Only time would tell. I forced cheer into my voice. "It's the phone records for the Varnado case."

"'Those aren't due until Monday, I thought."

How was Martina always so on top of everything? *Goals.* "Yeah, but I have a lot of homework, so I figured if I get this done earlier then I could spend the entire weekend studying."

"Smart, but don't work too hard. Is your workload here too much? We could scale back your hours if you need. How is school going?"

"Oh, no need for that. It's going well. It's busy and some of my business classes are so boring I wouldn't be surprised if you looked up boring in the dictionary and it listed the syllabus to my economics class, but some of my CJ classes are pretty cool." They were, but no classroom could mimic being on the job.

"How are things at your new apartment?"

Martina was one of the few people who knew where I actually lived since my employment record included my address. After Brendon died, I moved every six months in case the traffickers came after me. I mostly rented rooms with private entrances so that I could mount cameras without issue. So far there had been complete radio silence from the traffickers since Brendon's death. Maybe the network of traffickers figured I cleared my debt when they'd made good on their promise to kill Brendon, and the real revenge for them was that I had to live knowing it was my fault. *Smart.* I couldn't imagine a worse punishment.

"It's nice, but small. Although it's close to the beach, which is cool."

"Are you exercising regularly?"

I wondered if she'd noticed the weight I'd gained and the lackluster look in my eyes. "I've been running a few days a week, but haven't really hit the gym in a while. I met with Dee a couple of days ago. We went to the shooting range and then to dinner afterward. She's finally convinced me to join her at the Krav Maga studio. My first class is on Saturday."

A light shown in Martina's pale-brown eyes. "That's great, Selena. Remember, healthy body, healthy mind."

I nodded quietly. A bubble of emotion ran up my sinuses. I don't know why. Maybe I realized how much I missed talking to Martina. Now the only person I talked to about anything real was my therapist, which helped, but it wasn't family. I bit my lower lip. "How's Dad?"

"He is doing well. He misses you. Maybe you can come by the house for dinner this weekend?"

I wasn't sure that was smart, but I missed seeing them. "I'll check my schedule. If I don't have too much homework, maybe."

Sadness swept across her face. She placed her hand on my shoulder. "You know you're welcome anytime, Selena."

I averted my gaze. "Thanks, I know. I should really finish up these records so I can go home."

Martina's hand dropped back by her side. "Don't stay too late. I'm about to head out now too. Have a good night. I hope to see you this weekend."

I waved as she walked out. I pushed down all of my emotions and returned my focus to the computer screen displaying lists of numbers and letters. Now that I'd told Martina the Varnado files were the purpose for being in the office, I needed to finish them tonight. *Brilliant plan, Selena.*

9

TAYLOR

I BOUNCED DOWN THE HALL, EXCITED FOR THE DAY, HOPING to catch a glimpse of Dillon on the way to my next class. He looked adorable in class this morning. The wave in his hair and the white collar made him look like a male model. GQ or Abercrombie & Fitch. He was gorgeous. I could feel we were close to finally being together and starting our story. My heart skipped a beat at the sight of him near the exit of the building. Even in a sea of students, he stood out. I sped up to get closer and then stopped dead in my tracks. He was with her. Fire ran through my veins. There they stood within inches of one another, heads nearly touching as they spoke quietly, too quiet for me to hear. My hands curled into fists, my fingernails digging into the palms of my hands.

Why were they standing so close together? Why were they talking at all? Selena had sworn they weren't dating, and that she had no interest in dating him. So why the hell were they huddled up together?

I uncurled my fists and attempted to casually stroll past. Suddenly her demeanor changed as she tilted her head back and laughed at something Dillon must've said. Her hand was on his shoulder. Not dating? Not flirting? Not interested? Selena must think I'm some sort of idiot to believe her lies. I looked away and hurried past them, down the hall, pushing open the door to the outside. I sucked in the cool air, trying to catch my breath and trying not to lose my mind out in public, in front of everyone. Blood boiling, I looked left and right, looking for somewhere to go. Somewhere to get away. There were students and faculty in all directions. I broke out into a slight jog to get back to my dorm room as quickly, yet inconspicuously, as I could. I finally reached the door to my room and cursed as I fumbled with my keys to unlock the door.

Key in, I twisted the handle and pushed. No noise. Thank goodness my roommate, Mandy, was out. She would've asked what was wrong and I don't think I could've even talked about it. There was only one relief for me right now. I hurried to the bathroom, shutting the door behind me. I put my back against the wall and slid down as the defeat of the morning overwhelmed me. This could not be happening. She couldn't have him; he was meant for me. "For me!" I screamed to no one. What didn't Selena understand? Dillon was mine. Why couldn't she stay away? I had him right where I wanted him. Why did he look at her like that and not me? He had. That day at orientation. We had sparked. An actual connection. What happened? What was wrong with me? Why couldn't he love me? Why couldn't any man love me?

The pain in my chest intensified. I crawled over to the vanity with tears dripping on the floor. I pulled open my drawer and removed a small pink box with a gold etching of a rose on the cover. I set it down and slid down my jeans. I flipped the lid and retrieved a shiny razor blade. I brought it toward my inner thigh, fingertips shaking, I slid the blade down my tender flesh. Pain radiated from the wound and then I did another slit. I panted as I let the physical pain take over and the blood trickle.

My heart beat slowed and my breath calmed. I would be fine. I was fine.

A few minutes later, I wiped my eyes and lifted myself off the ground with the help of the vanity. I grabbed a tissue, dabbed the fresh cuts, and buttoned my jeans. I stared at myself in the mirror. Dillon had looked at me with those gorgeous blue eyes like he now looked at Selena. Is that what changed? Eyes wide, I said, "That's it. It's because of Selena. That's why he didn't call." He had been a little distracted by Selena and had forgotten. It's not that he didn't love me. It's that little miss investigator had stolen his attention. Well, she should know better than to take something that didn't belong to her. It looked like it would have to be me to remind her of that fact. Dillon and I were meant to be together and we would be together. *Any means necessary.*

10

SELENA

I stepped out of the gym and the wind hit me in the face, turning the sweat from my intense workout into little beads of ice. I pulled my fleece shut and zipped it up. "Well, looks like the weather turned." Dee chimed.

"Seriously. It is officially fall. Goodbye, sunshine."

"Yes, it only lasts so long. So what did you think of the workout? How did it feel?"

It kicked my butt, is what it did. I'd been running a few days a week, but I was definitely out of shape compared to before. That was dangerous and stupid. I couldn't believe I'd let myself go for so long without a proper workout regimen. "It was tough, but good."

Dee slapped me on the shoulder. "Keep coming back and don't you worry about it, you'll get your mojo back in no time."

Oh, how the student had surpassed the teacher. She was right. Boy, did it feel good to get in a hard workout like that. I would definitely keep coming back. Dee was able to get me a free membership for two weeks to try out the gym, and I intended to use it every single day. Oh, how I missed the high from a tough workout and the knowledge that I was getting stronger. It was a feeling I had nearly forgotten. "Thanks for bringing me, I feel great."

"Yeah, hey, what do you say we grab some breakfast?"

"I'm in."

"There's a great diner not too far from here that has an awesome veggie omelet. Perfect post-workout fuel."

"Sounds great."

Dee stopped in her tracks. "Hey, what happened to your car?"

I looked over at the driver's side of my vehicle and stopped cold. Someone had carved B-I-T-C-H into the driver's side door. I glanced back at Dee with a worried expression. "It wasn't there before we went into the gym."

She ran over to the car to inspect and glanced back at me. "Probably some punk kids did this. Teenagers."

I doubted it. Unless KT was a teenager or a punk kid. A dangerous one. She had followed me here and vandalized my car. She was escalating like Dee said she would.

Dee kneeled down and then stood back up. She turned around and said, "There's a note, Selena."

I rushed over to the car and grabbed the note off my windshield. Heart pounding, I read the very simple message.

DILLON IS MINE.
STAY AWAY OR YOU WILL BE SORRY.

I couldn't speak the words aloud. I handed the piece of paper to Dee.

I was now this deranged person's target. Dee's mouth dropped open. "Selena, this is bad. If you're dealing with somebody who's dangerous, you're now the target. This KT thinks you are standing in the way of her and Dillon. Why do you think she thinks that?"

"I'm not entirely sure. She's maybe seen me talking to him at school. I'm not doing anything with Dillon, other than trying to help him try to figure out who is sending him messages."

"Well, that's not what this person thinks, and now you're the target. You should make a police report to have a record. And..." She tipped her forehead at me. "You should call Martina."

Dee was right about one thing, a police report to document the evidence was a good idea, but I doubt the police would do much else and even if they did, they wouldn't be able to find anything. We'd already checked for IP addresses and phone numbers. There was no way this was KT's first stalking attempt. Not good news.

But if I called Martina, she'd know I'd kept this whole KT-Dillon thing a secret. I was only guiding him, not investigating. So maybe she wouldn't be mad? Or worse - disappointed. Dee stared at me as I stood there dumbfounded, contemplating what to do next. Before I could speak a word, she said, "Call Martina."

I let out a heavy sigh. "I'll call her."

Martina was so intimidating, even when I was just asking for help. I knew she would help, and I just had to suck it up because I needed her. "Hi, Martina."

I hesitated, still having difficulty getting the words out.

"Selena, are you still there? Is everything okay?"

Here goes. "Not exactly." I explained to her the entire story, from Dillon coming to me for help, to where I appeared to be the object of the stalker's attention. Martina was silent for what seemed like an eternity. There was nothing more terrifying than Martina when she was quiet.

Martina said, "You need to call the police to get a report. I'll come down there. It should take me about twenty minutes and then we can discuss how best to keep you and Dillon safe, okay?"

I tried to stop the tears. I tried to suppress the feeling that Martina was running to save me once again. It didn't matter if I pushed her away, she still came back whenever I needed her. I couldn't speak as I attempted to fight my tears. From the phone, I heard, "Selena, honey, it's going to be okay. Don't worry, we'll get this figured out."

"Okay," I choked.

"Ask Dee to stay with you if she can, okay?"

"I will, thank you, Martina."

"Anytime. I love you, Selena, and I'll be there soon."

I hung up and looked over at Dee as tears ran down my cheeks. She embraced me in a hug. I cried softly in Dee's arms for a full minute before I pushed back gently and wiped my face. "Sorry, I'm such a mess. I don't know what's happening with me anymore. Martina said she's coming down here and asked that you stay with me, if you can. I need to call the police to make a report."

"Of course, absolutely. I will stay with you." She put her hand on my shoulder. "Everything will be okay, Selena. Martina, the mighty lady warrior, will know how to handle it. This will all be okay."

I let out a soft chuckle at Dee's colorful, yet accurate, description of Martina. I believed Dee, and I believed Martina, but something told me this was far from over.

_____

11

TAYLOR

Not so tough now, are you, Selena? I smirked with satisfaction. I watched as her tall blonde friend hugged her as she cried. A twinge of guilt twisted inside of me. I hadn't wanted to hurt Selena or make her cry. I simply wanted her to stay away from Dillon. I had no other choice but to give her an explicit message to stay away from him. She hadn't responded appropriately to my text message, considering I saw them together the very next day. No, Selena apparently needed it to be loud and clear. Hopefully, she now understood, Dillon is mine, not hers, not anybody else's. I felt a little bad, but I couldn't let this person stand in the way of my and Dillon's happiness, could I?

I mean, nothing seemed bad about Selena and based on my research into her, she's had it rough and probably didn't deserve any of this, but like they say, all's fair in love and war. And I am a woman in love and I knew in my heart that Dillon would love me too, given the chance. He was just distracted by her, for *whatever* reason.

I sunk further into my passenger seat so that I could watch them from across the street. Now Selena was dialing somebody else on her phone. Probably the police. I figured as much considering her insurance would require a report to pay for the damages. But I'm no dummy. There's no way they'll be able to track it back to me.

It's not even that bad, although I do regret calling her a name. I don't really know her very well. She's probably not a bitch, but she needed to know that it was a targeted message just for her. Based on what I found about her online and her ex-boyfriend, well, her late boyfriend, she really should heed this warning and not get another person hurt, like herself.

I lowered my sunglasses to get a better look. As she spoke with more people outside of the gym, her tears dried and her expression changed from grief-stricken to a tired smile. Yes, Selena dear, you'll be just fine - that is, as long as you stay away from Dillon.

12

SELENA

"Why didn't you tell me what was going on?" The disappointment in Martina's eyes was almost too much for me to bear. I took a sip of my water and watched her closely before placing it back down on the table. She suggested we have brunch after the police came to take the report and promised to investigate the crime. I wasn't holding my breath they would find anything. Dee had politely exited the scene after Martina arrived, probably sensing that Martina and I needed some alone time. It was time to come clean about everything. Well, not everything. She didn't need to know about my continued investigation into the traffickers. Not that I'd gotten very far, therefore not much to tell. That was my story, and I was sticking to it.

I said, "I'm sorry I kept it from you. I tried to tell Dillon that I couldn't help because I needed to wait until I graduated college and had my PI license before I could investigate any more cases. I finally caved and said I'd help."

Martina leaned back against the vinyl booth. She unfolded her arms and lowered her head. She didn't speak for a few heartbeats before looking back up at me. "I apologize if I made you feel you couldn't come to me when you had a problem. Maybe I've been too strict about the requirements for me to recommend you for your private investigator's license, but I was trying to protect you. But maybe, I was also protecting your father and myself too. We'd be devastated if something were to happen to you. I know it's akin to torture sitting at a desk reviewing records all day. I get it. Trust me, I've been where you are."

I cocked my head. "Really?"

She nodded. "I've had my share of demons, and they landed me on probation. I don't want to get into the details right now. It was a long time ago, before I became a partner, but I remember it as if it were yesterday. When Stavros put me on probation, I felt like there was no purpose to what I was doing. I was bored, demoralized, and restless. I felt like a failure and that everything I did was wrong. Eventually, I realized it's okay to make mistakes as long as we learn from them."

I couldn't imagine what Martina could have done to get on the wrong side of Stavros. That was not a good place to be. Although, I don't think it differed greatly from being on the nasty side of Martina. "So what now?"

"You're three months from graduation, and for the last year and a half you've done nothing to cause me concern. I can't let you act officially on behalf of Drakos Monroe, but I'm okay with you taking on this case. I will support you in whatever you need, but it will have to be off the books."

My mouth dropped open, but I quickly closed it.

Martina continued. "There is one condition."

I nodded.

"If it ever looks like you're in danger or you could be, let me know. Immediately. I need you to promise me."

I let go of the breath I didn't realize I'd been holding. I really wanted to stay strong and not cry. I didn't want to look weak to Martina. I wanted her to know I was serious. She was giving me a lifeline, an olive branch. I'd investigate by the book and let her know what was going on and if it appeared too dangerous. I wasn't completely convinced it would be. I mean, sure, there was some vandalism and gifts, but to date nothing violent. "I promise."

Martina nodded her approval. "I'm glad to hear that. I know I can't always protect you. You're getting older and soon you'll have your license and a college degree. Speaking of, have you thought about what you want to do after graduation?"

The more I thought about it, the more I was sure I wanted to stay in private investigations. I liked the idea of having the freedom to run my own investigations and be my own boss. I wasn't sure how Martina would take the news that I'd likely be leaving Drakos Monroe. "Well, I'm about 99% sure I want to stay in private investigations and not go into law enforcement."

A grin spread across Martina's face. "That's great. I'm thrilled to hear that. I think it suits you. But why the serious face?"

I really needed to learn how to read people like Martina could. "It's just that I was thinking maybe I'd like to be independent. Be my own boss and maybe have my own firm. Obviously it would be a one woman show for a while but, yeah, I think that's what I want." I braced myself for her reaction.

Martina's smile faded. "I see. Have you started looking into what it would take to run your own business and get started?"

It wasn't the response I had expected. She didn't seem angry, more surprised, and maybe a little disappointed. I wasn't quite sure, I wasn't a master at reading other people's emotions - not yet anyways. "Actually, yes. I'm learning so much in my business classes; it's how I got the idea. Last semester, I took a class on entrepreneurship and was really fascinated. We even had to create a business plan for our final, so technically I have at least a draft business plan for my future company."

"You seem excited about it."

"I am."

"I'm happy for you. And when the time comes to get started, I hope you know you can come to me and I'll help in any way I can."

"That would be great. Thank you."

I wasn't sure what I had done to deserve a stepmother like Martina. I really tried to stay tough, but I didn't think I could hold back any longer. My eyes misted, and I shook my head, wiping under my eyes. "I'm so sorry I didn't come to you before."

Now that the waterworks were on full blast, I grabbed my napkin from on top of the table and tried to calm myself as I sobbed into my napkin. Martina slid next to me, placing her arm around my shoulders. I don't know why I was breaking down. It was as if the last eighteen months were pouring out of me. The loneliness. The guilt. The sadness. Missing Dad and Martina and the life I had before Brendon died. I sat up and did a final dabbing of my eyes.

Martina stroked the back of my hair. "Honey, you've made some mistakes in the past, and you will make some in the future. No matter what those mistakes are, I will always be here for you. You know that, right?"

If she was trying to make me cry less, she was failing miserably. I nodded before wrapping my arms around her. After a few long moments, we both sat back. Martina used the tip of her finger to dab at the edges of her eyes, and I used my soaked napkin for my dripping eyes. I exhaled. "Thank you for everything."

"You're very welcome. What do you say we splurge and get some strawberry waffles?"

Waffles with Martina. Now, that was something I could get used to.

13

SELENA

I rapped my knuckles on Dillon's front door. I quietly reminded myself to focus on the case. *Just the case.* The door creaked open and a worried-looking Dillon appeared. His hands shook as he held onto the edge of the door and opened it so that I could enter his apartment. I surveyed the small apartment before I refocused on Dillon. "Hi."

"Come on in." He said.

I stepped into the apartment which was cool and had a musty scent. Boy scent. "Everything okay?"

"No, not everything is okay. I want to show you something." He didn't wait for me to respond. Instead, he hurried down the hallway and then turned to the first door on the left. His bedroom. I didn't think he was being forward, but just in case, I approached cautiously, one baby step at a time. On top of the bed sat a box of See's candy. Had he lured me in here with candy? He barely knew me. How did he know that would work? *Kidding.* It would take a lot more than candy to get me into his bed, or any man's bed.

He stood next to the bed and picked up a note that sat on

top of a white box with black and gold lettering. "I found this when I got home today." He handed the folded note to me.

I unfolded it.

SWEETS FOR MY SWEET.

Another gift from KT. "Where did you find this?"

He wiped his hands on his jeans. "On my bed. Right there." He pointed to the box of chocolates sitting on the bed.

"Have you asked your roommate about it?"

"He's not home, but I texted him. He hasn't been home all day and knows nothing about it."

Not a good sign. The stalker texted him, emailed him, followed him, announced on Facebook that they were in a relationship, vandalized my car, threatened me to stay away from Dillon, and now broke into his apartment. This was really not good. Now I understood why Dillon was so visibly upset. He must feel so violated, knowing somebody had entered his apartment. Break-in's often broke not only a door or window, but the false sense of safety and security people had in their own homes. "Have you touched the box?"

"I haven't touched it."

"I think you should call the police. She broke into your apartment. At the very least, the police will take a report so we have a history, plus they might get fingerprints. And then we can continue our investigation and make this all stop once and for all."

He shook his head, not understanding what I was saying. "Our own investigation? I thought you couldn't?"

I smirked. I hadn't told him the news that Martina was allowing me to take his case. "It's one thing I wanted to discuss with you. I had a heart-to-heart with my stepmother, Martina, after my car was vandalized. I told her everything about your situation. She told me she'd support me in investigating the case. It's not an official Drakos Monroe case, but I can help in any way I can. The first step is getting fingerprints, so let's call the police to get a record and maybe prints. We will find out KT's identity and we will make her stop."

Dillon's body relaxed. "That's awesome news. I don't have a lot of money, but I can help with some expenses. I'm not sure which ones but ... I don't even know how much things cost."

"Let's just take it one step at a time. If the police's fingerprint analysis doesn't come back soon, we will have to do it ourselves. Speaking of, call them. It'll probably take a while for them to get there. While we're waiting, let's go over all the information you have so far and then we'll talk next steps. How does that sound?"

He raked his fingers through his hair. "Good. Thank you, Selena. I really appreciate you helping me. This whole situation is really freaking me out."

No doubt. We needed to catch KT and make her leave Dillon alone.

After the police left the apartment and a mess of gray fingerprint dust lay all over the place, I sat down at the small dining table with Dillon and we printed out all the emails, texts, and IP address locations from his laptop. We pored over the records and strategized over everything we could glean about KT.

Next thing for us to do was to catch her in the act and reveal her identity once and for all. That was where I'd come in. I had a plan, and it was going to work. I felt bad for Dillon, but I also felt like I'd been awoken from a deep sleep. It was sunrise, and I was ready for everything the day had in store. I hoped KT was ready too, because I was coming for her.

14

DILLON

I watched Selena as she waved her hands in the air and explained to me all the things she would do to help me figure out who KT really was and to make all of this madness stop. I followed her obediently as she strode around my apartment showing me all the vulnerable entry points and where I should add cameras to help catch KT in the act as well as a few inexpensive alarms that would alert if an intruder were to open a door or window.

This whole KT thing had me pretty shook. I never thought I'd fear some girl, assuming KT was a girl. It was all freaking me out. It was too strange to comprehend. I don't know how I would sleep in my bed tonight. I glanced over at the couch in the living room. Selena continued to name different models of in-home security cameras I should consider. I couldn't really think of that right now. I was more concerned about where I'd sleep tonight - maybe on the couch. Would that be better than my room? At least my bedroom had a door I could lock. Selena stopped talking and stared me in the eye. "What? Am I talking too fast?"

"No, not at all, you really know your cameras." She was

amazing. She was smart. She was beautiful. She was unique. I've never met anybody like her. We continued like this until we got to my bedroom. She pointed at my window and opened and closed it to see how secure it was. I glanced at my bed, now free of the tainted chocolates.

I don't know how my brain could nearly immediately shift to images of Selena lying there, waiting for me. I really needed to squash those thoughts. How could I switch from anxiety triggered by a faceless threat to lusting after a beautiful, intriguing woman? As my psych professors often explained, the brain was a fascinating and complex thing capable of many conflicting thoughts and ideas. Compartmentalization.

Maybe Selena was distracting me from the fear of the unknown KT? And maybe that was a good thing.

After Selena's assessment, we exited my bedroom into the hallway. The creaking of the front door opening stopped me in my tracks. Selena stepped ahead of me, glanced back and whispered. "Stay here, I'll check it out."

She continued slowly, like a cat barely making a noise. I watched her from behind. It wasn't an unpleasant view. She turned the corner. "Wow. Hey, who are you?"

I let go of the breath I'd been holding.

"I'm Selena. You are?"

"Dude. I'm Ryan, I live here."

I walked out. "Hey, Ryan. This is Selena, she's here because we had a break-in earlier."

He gave me a quizzical look like 'you let some small girl protect you from a potential intruder?' I suppose he had a point. "Oh, seriously, bro? Did they take anything?"

"No, more like they left something."

Ryan squished up his face. "Uh, like something dead?"

Based on Selena's and my behavior, his thought wasn't completely odd. Candy didn't seem nearly as scary as say coming home to find a pet bunny cooking on the stove. "No, it was KT. She broke in and left a box of chocolates."

"Were they poisoned?"

Were we making too big a deal out of the chocolates? No, we weren't. She broke into the apartment. It was escalating. It was good to be cautious. "Not that we know of." Although I hadn't planned to eat them, it was a good thing to consider.

Ryan glanced at Selena and then back at me. "Okay. So..."

"Selena is an investigator, she's helping me find out who KT is so she'll stop all the notes and gifts and posting on social media. She suggested we put up cameras and alarms."

"Not in my room, right, bro?"

I looked at Selena. "We don't have to, it's just a precaution. If we can get her on video, we can figure out who she is. If you aren't comfortable with it, we can skip your room."

"That's probably best. You don't want to see what goes on in there." He tittered.

Selena eyed him like she wasn't impressed. "Anyway, it was nice to meet you, Ryan. Dillon, you and I will talk later. I'll email you all my recommendations for the cameras and alarms."

She waved at both of us and exited.

Both Ryan and I watched as she walked out. I shut the door and turned around to face my roommate. He was covering his wide grin. He waved his arm in front of him. "Damn bro, she is fine. Are you making up all of this KT stuff to get her into your bed? I wouldn't blame you. No judgements." He chortled.

He was such an idiot. "No, that's not what's going on. She's helping me stop this person. They broke into our apartment. That's not normal."

"Hey, hey. No need to get defensive. I'm just teasing you, bro. Wait, did you call the cops?"

"Yes. They were here earlier. I didn't see any of my stuff

missing, but they suggested I ask you to check to see if anything of yours was missing."

"Did the cops go in my room?"

"Just a quick walk-through to make sure nobody was hiding out."

"Did they go through my stuff?"

"No, like I said, just a walk-through."

"Cool, bro. You had me worried for a sec."

It was going to be a long year with bro. Time to go order cameras and an alarm. Hopefully, I had enough money in my bank account. KT was not only costing me my sanity but a bucket-load of money too.

15

SELENA

I slipped into a small conference room with my laptop tucked under my arm. Now that I had two hush-hush investigations I was working, it was better to situate myself behind closed doors when I was in the office.

I sat at the end of the table with my computer in front of me in order to have a view of anyone walking by or toward the conference room. Martina said it was fine that I used company computers and resources to help Dillon because I was simply helping Dillon and wasn't being compensated.

She still didn't know I was looking into the traffickers. Not that I'd been able to find much. One of my main issues was that the only information I had was a few names, and all were deceased or in jail, which made it trickier since there weren't any movements to track. The only genuine lead I had was following the money in their bank accounts, but of course both estates had been tied up in probate for over a year. It was a dead end - for now. Almost as dead as Ocampo and his friend.

You weren't supposed to speak ill of the dead, but I was glad Ocampo was gone. He was the one who threatened me. He was the one I'd met face-to-face. He was the man who was using a nail salon as a cover to traffic women who were held against their will, barely fed, and forced to live in a back room on mattresses on the floor. If that wasn't bad enough, they were also forced to service not only wealthy clients by scrubbing their feet and clipping their cuticles but also by catering to the men who came through the back door in the evening and sometimes boldly during the day. It was sickening and disgusting, and Ocampo seem to thrive on it. I didn't shed a tear for him when Martina gave him a bullet as a parting gift. I didn't know the other guy that was killed, but since he was working with Ocampo I'm sure he deserved Martina's bullet just as much.

I opened the lid of my laptop and skimmed through my emails. Nothing urgent. Time to investigate KT. I reread all the reports on KT's phone number and IP addresses Dillon had secured. I reran them using our system to make sure all the information was accurate. It was. *Bummer.*

I studied the physical addresses associated with the IP addresses and pulled up a map online. *Hmm. Interesting.* All the locations were on campus, with the overwhelming majority at the main library. Since the emails and Facebook posts were never accessed off campus, I'd bet money it wasn't staff or faculty. KT had to be a student. And to use school computers you had to put in your student ID. I wondered if the library would give me a list of student logins over the past month. It would be important so that I could catch her while she was posting or emailing Dillon. It was time for a good old-fashioned stakeout. My adrenaline was pumping. I'd be back out there on a case, not just behind the desk, staring at numbers and letters on a screen. *I am back.*

I might have this case wrapped up in three days, five tops. I sunk into my shoulders. And then what? Another few months of reviewing records, studying, going to classes — in other words back to Boringsville. I pushed the dreadful thoughts away and tapped out a few notes for my next steps and closed out the file.

I glanced up and didn't see anyone near the conference room. I opened up the financial database I'd been using to track Ocampo and his partner's estate. Both of their homes, and the nail salon owned by Ocampo, were still on the market and no movement on the bank accounts. I had nothing, and it wasn't quite time for my weekly call to the police who were supposedly investigating the case. Not that they ever really gave me any details. It was always the same, "I'm sorry ma'am, we can't give out details of an ongoing investigation." I called BS. I doubt they had much more than I did. Unless, of course, they were staking out the families, but from what I understood, the wives and children did not know about their spouse's double lives. Both were supposedly pillars of the community that attended church and little league games.

A knock on the door made me jump and quickly close my current window. I glanced above my laptop. I waved. "Burning the midnight oil?" Martina asked.

"I could say the same to you."

"Touche. Mind if I join you?"

"Sure. I was just doing a bit of work."

Martina strolled in and sat herself down on the chair across from me.

"Any fresh developments in Dillon's case?"

I told her what had happened the day before at his apartment and described my current plan to uncover KT's identity. She seemed pleased; I figured if I received Martina's seal of approval, it must be a good plan. "What has you working late? You must be on some big case if you're working on the weekend." I asked.

"New case. A missing girl, a high school senior planning to attend SFU, but vanished the night of graduation."

"I don't remember hearing about that. Where is she from?"

"Walnut Creek."

My gut stirred. "Which school did she attend?"

"I would have to check the file, it was one of the public schools. She was supposed to be picked up after grad night, but when her parents arrived at the school the next morning, she was gone. Witnesses say that the last time they saw her, she'd said her ride was there, and she ran off toward the parking lot. They all assumed her ride was her parents, but nobody ever saw her again."

"That's strange. Nobody saw anything?"

"So they say."

"Did anyone know if she was having any problems with a boyfriend or drugs or mental health?"

Martina seemed to suppress a smile. She must've missed having these conversations with me too.

"At first glance, Kaitlyn had a pretty normal life. Friends, good grades, no drugs or serious boyfriends. She had been accepted to SFU and was going to start in the fall with her best friend. We haven't talked to her best friend yet. I just have the statements from the police who didn't seem to take it too seriously at first, thought Kaitlyn was out celebrating her graduation. They didn't even start a search until the next day."

Which in a missing persons case is a long, freakin' time. "She's been missing for almost four months? Somebody has to know what happened to her. The police can't possibly think she's still celebrating or a runaway."

"I think they've moved on from those theories, but they have little to go on and I agree, someone knows something. That's where we come in. It's our - or my job to find that someone and bring Kaitlyn home."

I chewed my lower lip as I contemplated the missing person case. Walnut Creek? Where had I just heard that?

"What is it?" Martina asked.

"It may be a coincidence, but I recently met someone from Walnut Creek. A girl in my economics class. A freshman."

Martina's eyebrows jutted up. "What is her name? What do you know about her?"

"Her name is Taylor, she's a tall blonde. Wide-eyed, optimistic, friendly, maybe a little on the insecure side. Could be because she's young and away from home for the first time."

Martina's expression hardened. "Would you be willing to talk to Taylor and ask her if she knew Kaitlyn?"

Yes. I would very much like to help you in your investigation. "I suppose. I have class with her tomorrow. Do you think she may know Kaitlyn?"

"Taylor is a fairly common name, but I don't want to tell you too many details yet. I would like to you to ask her some questions and to get your unbiased opinion of her answers. Is that okay?"

I couldn't help but smile. Martina trusted me and wanted my input on an important case. "Yeah, that's totally fine. I get it, it makes sense."

"Great. I was about to head out. Your dad is making enchiladas if you want to come over?"

I had wanted to see my dad, but I also had work to do. I suppose I could take the night off. There was nothing new with Ocampo, I had a plan for KT, and I was working on one of Martina's cases. Actually, enchiladas sounded freaking great.

"I'm in."

I packed up my things with a renewed sense of self. It felt so good to have a purpose and to be doing something that I thought could help somebody else, actually now multiple somebodies. Things were definitely looking up.

THE WOMAN NEXT TO ME SIGHED. I TURNED TO FIGURE OUT what was causing her displeasure. "What's wrong?"

She held up her paper displaying a 71 written in red marker. "71, that is barely passing. I can't be barely passing in my major." She looked over at my paper and sunk into herself. "Well, you seem to have no problem understanding supply and demand. You wouldn't want to maybe tutor me? I'd buy lunch."

She had wide eyes and a smile. I wasn't convinced she was all that broken up over the grade. "Do you really need a tutor or do you maybe just need to study more?"

"I don't know, maybe a little of both. You're probably right, but I think it would help to have a study buddy. You know, someone who's going to get me to sit down and crack open the book and do the work. Would you be my study buddy? Offer for lunch still stands."

Was she doing this so I'd go out with her? She was cute, bubbly, but awfully young. She was over-eager and excited and barely passing a very easy class. "So what did you have in mind?"

She clapped her hands together lightly. "So you'll do it. Oh, thank you so much. How about Friday? There's a cool café where I see tons of people studying and having lunch. The food and beverage options look great. Hydration is important." She chimed.

She sure was full of enthusiasm. Gosh, I just wished that I didn't have a stalker, and I could sleep in my own bed at night and not worry about someone breaking in to give me candy. Okay, when I thought about it like that it sounded a little silly. But if it was just silly why was the situation driving me mad?

I looked into Taylor's bright blue eyes and smiled. She was certainly no Selena, but maybe she could be a distraction from my thoughts about Selena. I really needed to stop thinking about Selena in that way. She was helping me and I couldn't cross that line - it didn't feel right. Maybe after the case? I shrugged. "Sure, why not?"

"Thank you so much." She hesitated as she looked above my shoulder. Her face appeared to have melted. Her eyes squinted, and a frown replaced her beaming smile.

I instinctively looked over my shoulder. "Oh, hey, Selena."

"Hi, Dillon. Hi, Taylor."

"Were we supposed to meet today?" I asked.

She shook her head. "No, actually I came over to see if I could talk to Taylor."

I looked over at Taylor's expression. It softened a smidge. Did she not want to talk to Selena? In a flash, Taylor perked up in her seat. "Of course, when did you have in mind?"

"Now if you have a few minutes?"

"Sure, I just have to pack up my things."

Selena smiled. "Great."

I watched as Taylor packed up her bag. I stood up and exited the row to allow her to comfortably leave. She stood and met Selena.

Taylor waved, and then exited the auditorium with Selena. I watched as they walked. Taylor had a great figure, but was she more than what you saw on the surface? Did she have a deeper side — and the ditzy persona was just an act? She seemed to be more intelligent when we'd first met at orientation. We discussed grabbing lunch, and she gave me her number. I had put her out of my mind though; she seemed okay enough, just a little young.

I continued to watch them as they strolled out. They were opposite in looks Selena was petite, curvy, gorgeous with chestnut-colored hair. Taylor was tall, lean, blonde. Both cute, but one was edgy and the other not so much. Taylor was more of a distraction than a potential girlfriend, I supposed, whereas Selena was a muse. A creature that made you want to live your best life with her by your side. *Dang it.* I needed to get a grip, this whole KT business was making me nuts.

17

SELENA

I wrapped my scarf around my neck as Taylor and I exited the building. "Thank you for agreeing to talk with me. I really appreciate it."

Taylor bounced beside me. "No biggie. What did you want to ask?"

She sure was bubbly for this early in the morning. I wasn't typically anywhere near bubble status until I had at least two cups of coffee. "Do you mind if we walk and talk? I need to go to the library."

"No problem. I could definitely use the exercise." She chuckled. "What you do for exercise? You seem super fit."

Not enough. "I run and I started up with Krav Maga again."

"Wow, super intense, isn't it? I don't think I could handle it."

"It's not for the faint of heart. I used to be in great shape, and then I kind of fell out of it. I recently started back at the gym. It was time."

"So... what was it you wanted to talk to me about?"

"Well, I don't know if you know this or not, I don't know how you would. I actually work for a private investigation and security firm. Drakos Monroe. Have you heard of it?"

I glanced sideways to see how she reacted to the information.

"No, can't say that I have."

"Well." I paused as I waved at Dee, who was walking toward us. "Hey Dee."

"Hey Selena, in a rush, but can we talk later today?"

"Sure, I'll text you later." I said.

It was nice to be seeing Dee regularly; it was mostly for gym and shooting dates, but it was nice to have her back in my life. I jogged up the steps to the front of the library. "Sorry, I was saying..." I opened the door and ushered her in ahead of me. "I work for this firm and my stepmother, who is part owner, had asked me if I could ask you about a missing person she's investigating that is also from Walnut Creek."

"Really?"

I surveyed the library and spotted an open table. I pulled out a heavy wooden chair with faded cloth seating and sat down before placing my backpack on the carpet. I unzipped it and pulled out my notebook that I used for my work at Drakos Monroe. I flipped it open and clicked my pen. "Yes, I was talking to my stepmother, and I recalled you telling me you were from Walnut Creek. I mentioned it to my stepmom, and she asked me to talk to you about it."

She scooted the chair closer to the table and lifted her sculpted eyebrows. "Really? Walnut Creek's not a big town. What's the persons's name?"

"Her name is Kaitlyn Wilkes. Did you know her?"

Taylor's face melted, and she shook her head as if it weren't possible.

"You knew her?" I asked.

"Yeah. I, uh, I hadn't heard she was missing."

"How did you know her?"

"We'd been friends for a long time."

"You went to the same high school?"

"Same middle school and high school. We were good friends. Best friends - for a time."

"But you didn't know she'd been missing?"

Taylor shifted her gaze to the floor. "I mean, I hadn't heard from her and the police had asked if I'd seen her after Grad night, but..."

"So you knew she was missing?"

She looked back up at me. "No, I mean, I know they thought she was missing. I assumed she'd simply snuck away with her boyfriend."

"Did you know him too? Do you know his name?"

"Not exactly. First name Greg, didn't catch the last name. He was older and from what I could tell was kinda gross. We never hung out."

"How long had they been dating?"

"Not long. A few months, I think." Taylor looked back at the ground as she chewed her bottom lip. "I haven't heard from her."

Interesting bit of info I hadn't asked for. "Is that strange not to have heard from her?"

"She'd been spending a lot of time with Greg and..."

"And what?"

"Nothing, really. I didn't like him and so she started to spend less time with me and more time with him."

"Why didn't you like him?"

Taylor shrugged. "I only met him once. I got bad vibes from him. He was too, I don't know, too clingy and controlling. He showered her with texts and compliments constantly and wanted to spend every moment with her. She loved it, but I thought it was weird."

My heart sunk. If what Taylor said was true, this was not great news. Greg sounded like a potentially abusive partner, which means he could have Kaitlyn stashed somewhere. Shivers ran down my spine with thoughts of Zeek. How stupid I'd been to think I'd found my perfect guy and not a murdering monster. I wondered if Kaitlyn thought she'd found herself the perfect boyfriend too.

I scribbled a few notes into my notebook.

"What's wrong?" Taylor asked.

"Oh nothing, your story about Kaitlyn and Greg reminded of a similar situation."

"A bad one?"

"To put it lightly. Yes, bad." Bad like he kidnapped me and tried to kill me. Like he'd killed other girls before me. I shook the memories away and refocused on Taylor. I studied her features. Pretty. Young. She seemed to be telling the truth, but it also seemed like she was holding back.

"When was the last time you saw Kaitlyn?"

"Grad night. I saw her leave with Greg."

What? Martina had said that according to the police reports, the last sightings were of her running off to what they assumed was Kaitlyn's parents' car.

"Did you say anything to her?"

"Like what?"

"Good bye? Talk later?" I suggested.

"No." Taylor had shifted her gaze away from me and down to her hand. She wiggled her fingers and her nail polish glittered in the light overhead.

"Were you in a fight?"

Taylor stared at the table. Pain in her eyes. "We got into a fight that night. She told me - she said some mean things and then said our friendship was over."

"What was the fight about?"

"I don't really remember. Something about how she was starting fresh or something." Taylor said rather quickly.

Don't remember what the fight was about? I'm not sure I

bought it, but based on Taylor's demeanor, it was upsetting her so I didn't push. "Do you think it is out of character for Kaitlyn to run off with him and to skip out on going to college?" I stared straight into her eyes, looking for a sign of concern over her former best friend's wellbeing.

Her eyes grew wide with concern, and her mouth dropped open.

"What?"

"You said she was missing. I suppose it hadn't dawned on me that she hadn't been in school. No, it's not like her. She had big dreams of being a lawyer and moving to New York." Taylor threw her hands to her face and started heaving. She began muttering something before looking back up. "It didn't occur to me something bad could've happened with that guy. My God, I should call her parents and ask how they're doing. Anything you need for the investigation, I'm here to help - with anything at all. I'll give you all the information I have. Any old messages - like I said, I haven't heard from her since grad night. Oh, my gosh. I've been so stupid. I should've realized that maybe something was wrong. I'm such an idiot. I can't believe I'm such an idiot, and I totally missed this. I hope she's okay. I mean, do you think she's okay?"

Taylor seemed to have unraveled before my eyes. "I hope so."

"Your stepmom, is she good at finding people?"

I gave a lopsided grin. "Great at it." She'd found me and saved my life.

"Please let me know if I can help." Taylor pleaded.

"I'll let you know if I hear anything. I'll give my notes to Martina and see how it fits. But look, I gotta go. If there's anything else that you can think of that might help us find Kaitlyn, will you let me know?"

Taylor nodded furiously. "Of course. If anything comes to mind, I'll definitely let you know."

"Are you okay?"

Taylor wiped a tear from her eye. "Yes, I'm fine. I'll be okay. Thank you."

"I have to talk to the librarian about something. I'll see you later, okay?"

She nodded, and I stuffed my notebook into my backpack. Were her tears real? The switch from bubbly to devastated was so fast. I wondered how it all fit. It would be interesting to compare notes with Martina. Did the investigators know Kaitlyn had a potentially abusive boyfriend?

18

SELENA

I POLITELY LAUGHED AT HIS UMPTEENTH OFF-COLOR JOKE of the lunch. When he finished his latest terrible joke, I sipped my coffee and set it back down. "Wow, Van. This has been great. It was nice to meet another person on campus. I really appreciate all of your help." Without this creep I wouldn't have gotten the library computer login record for the last month, which was critical to my KT investigation.

"Are you sure you can't stay for some dessert? If you don't like what's on the menu, maybe I have something you'd like back at my place." He wiggled his brows.

Ick. "Sorry, but I have to meet my stepmother. She gets really mad if I'm late, and I don't want her to be mad at me." This lunch had taken a strange turn. Sure, it wasn't totally cool that I'd used my feminine wiles to get some information out of this person but I thought he was an okay guy. I supposed I should've known he was terrible when he'd told me he was only willing to give me the records if I agreed to go out to lunch with him.

"Maybe another time. I have a feeling you have a sweet tooth and I've got just the treat for you." He said with a smirk.

Double ick.

I glanced up at the server who set the check down on the table. Thank goodness he had arrived. I watched as Van picked it up and looked at it. Van didn't strike me as someone who would treat a lady on the first date, but maybe his weird gross vibe was just a facade and on the inside he was a perfect gentleman. He set it back down and reached in his back pocket for his wallet. "My half is twelve bucks, yours was eight. We each pay for what we ordered, cool?"

No, he was a sleazeball jerk-face inside and out. Thank goodness I had cash with me so I wouldn't have to wait for the credit card to be processed. I grabbed a twenty from my wallet, which would provide the server with a well-deserved tip after having to deal with Van's rude comments and disgusting behavior. Dillon really owed me for putting me through this. Suddenly my thoughts drifted back to my lunch with Dillon. Dillon was the opposite of this creep. Sweet, funny, driven, and well, was being stalked. Not all great things. I grabbed my backpack and threw it over my shoulder. "Thanks. Bye." I didn't wait for a response, instead I rushed out of the restaurant and headed towards my car. I felt like I had a layer of slime covering me from head to toe. I was going to need at least two showers to wash off the *ick* that was Van-the-librarian.

I STEPPED INTO THE WAITING AREA OF THE SAN FRANCISCO Police Department. I hadn't been there for a few years, but it still had the same dusty smell. I spotted Martina in the corner speaking to a man with a familiar shiny bald head. The man who helped me take down the fraternity house after it was discovered that they were sexually assaulting women on campus and getting away with it, thanks to a jerky on-campus cop.

When I explained to Martina what was happening at the DKA house and shown her the proof I had, she brought it to Lt. Tippin. He believed Martina and acted fast.

My smile widened as I reached out my hand to Lt. Tippin. His firm shake exuded confidence and strength.

"Great to see you, Selena. How have you been?"

I release my hand and stuck it in the front pocket of my hoodie. "Okay. I'm graduating soon. I'm sure Martina explained, I'm here trying to help out a friend, a classmate who had his apartment broken into. My friend is having a hard time getting anybody to answer the phone."

"Who was the responding officer?"

"Heller."

Tippin's face went stone-cold. "I'll take you to him. I'll make sure he gives you whatever you need."

Lt. Tippin was a hero in my book. An officer sworn to serve and protect, and he did just that. We walked and talked about school and my future plans. "Any thoughts of joining us in law enforcement?"

Martina and Tippin's eyes were on me. "I've thought about it, but there's something about private investigations that really intrigues me."

Tippin smirked. "I think it's that you like to play by your own rules, am I right?"

I really needed to work on my people-reading skills. And my poker face. Tippin and Martina had my number. "Something like that, but I do like working alongside with the police."

He tipped his chin. "You know we use consultants from time to time. Who knows, maybe we'll be working together in a few years."

"Really? I'd love to hear more about that."

"My office is always open to you, Selena, and of course to you too, Martina."

We approached the desk of a uniformed officer with dark brown hair and a 5 o'clock shadow. He glanced up at the three of us and stiffened. He focused his gaze on Lt. Tippin, "LT, what can I do for you?"

Tippin remained stoic. "Glad you asked. I'd like to introduce you to a couple of very good friends of mine. To the right here is Ms. Martina Monroe and her stepdaughter Selena Bailey. Selena has been helping a friend of hers who had a break-in where you were the responding officer. I need you to give her any information that she asks for. Are we clear?"

"Of course, yes, sir."

Tippin turned to me, gave me a wink and patted Martina on the shoulder. "You two take care. It's been great seeing you. Stop in and say good-bye before you leave."

After introductions, Officer Heller gave a nervous smile and sat back down. "What was the name of your friend who had the break-in?"

I was relaying all the details of Dillon's break-in when, from the corner of my eye, I spotted a familiar face. My heart sped up and I couldn't look away. All my memories flooded back to that day. The pity on his face. The tissues that he handed me. The calm voice that became white noise as my mind exited the building.

"Ms. Bailey, Ms. Bailey?"

I felt a hand on my shoulder and stared up at Martina. Our eyes locked and my chest heaved. "What is it, Selena?"

I couldn't speak. I watched as she glanced over my shoulder before returning her gaze to me. "Stay here. I'll be right back."

We weren't here on official business, but knew a direct order when I heard it.

I returned my attention back to Officer Heller. "I'm sorry, I just saw someone I've worked with in the past." Worked with might be a stretch. He was investigating Brendon's murder. "Have you run the prints yet?"

"Yeah, we came back with nothing. The only prints we found were of your friend and his roommate. Whoever broke in must've worn gloves, and from our inspection looks like they probably climbed in through an open window. Only one window in the apartment had been locked."

I glanced back over at Detective Brown, who was engrossed in a conversation with Martina. "So you have nothing?"

"Sorry, I wish I could be more helpful. If anything comes up, I'll let you know. I'll run a search to see if there have been any other break-in's in the area that may be related."

I knew it wasn't a string of burglaries, this guy was an idiot. "Thanks, that would be great."

He reached over his desk and pulled a white business card with the city's emblem in the left-hand corner and handed to me. "Call me if you need anything."

"Thanks." I turned around and headed towards Martina and Detective Brown.

Martina stopped when she saw that I was within earshot. She reintroduced the two of us, even though I could tell by the look in Detective Brown's eyes, he knew exactly who I was. I was the person who called him weekly since Brendon's death. What was one more time? "Any developments in Brendon's case?"

He nodded. "I was just telling Martina there has been a recent development." My heartbeat sped up. I didn't let him finish his sentence. "Have you found the people who were above Ocampo?"

He lifted his hand in protest. "I can't tell you a lot, but what I can tell you is that we have a new lead that we're following. It seems to be credible. That is all I can tell you right now."

I glanced over at Martina as if she'd be able to tell me if he was telling the truth or not. She gave me a reassuring nod. "There's absolutely nothing else you can tell me?" I asked again.

"When I have anything else I can share, I will."

"You now have my contact information and I know you have Selena's. We'd appreciate a call if there are any breaks in the case - before the press gets a hold of it." Martina demanded, in her typical badass way.

She thanked him for his time before we silently exited the station. So many thoughts were swirling in my mind. I was mad. I was frustrated. There was a break in the case and I didn't know what it was. I wondered what they'd found. I may need to get creative to figure it out. I should head back to the office and check the databases to see if I could piece together what the police had found. I wanted to help get Brendon's killers off the streets and stop them from hurting anybody else ever again. I would get justice for Brendon and those women if it was the last thing I did.

Martina stopped when we reached the entrance to the parking lot. "Are you okay?"

I needed to hang around with less intuitive people if I was going to effectively conceal my feelings. "It's just..."

"You think about it a lot, don't you?"

I nodded as I stared at the concrete.

"Look at me."

I glanced up and met her warm, caring eyes.

"What happened was horrific and I know it's difficult to let go, but if you don't, it will eat away at you until there's nothing left. He wouldn't want that. You know that."

I hated when she was so right. But he would want me to get justice for him and the other victims. "You're right." I said, hoping it would end the conversation. I didn't want to give away that I was still searching for the higher ups in the organization, those that were still running free.

"And I want you to let the police do their job. They have a full task force still working the case. It's too dangerous for you to be involved. You know this, right?"

I looked confidently into her brown eyes. "I know." I seethed. I didn't always enjoy the preachy side of Martina. The one who always knew better. Which, to be fair, she usually did, but I didn't have to like it. I knew searching for the traffickers was dangerous. It was the entire reason I'd been keeping people away from me.

Tension filled the space between us.

"Good. Now, what's your next step for helping Dillon?"

My body relaxed. "Well, I just sat through a very painful lunch with a creeper who works at the library. In exchange for the hour of my life, that I'll never get back, he gave me a list of computer logins for the last month."

Martina raised an eyebrow. "Not exactly legal."

"Well, I'm not taking anyone to court, I'm hoping to find a pattern between logins and the timing of emails and Facebooks posts from KT."

"And then stakeout the library?"

"Exactly. I need to study anyway. Two birds."

"Anything you need from me?" Martina asked.

"Nope. I've got it covered."

"Then I'll see you in the office Wednesday?"

You betcha, I had work to do on Brendon's case. "Yep. Oh, I nearly forgot. It's been a busy day. I spoke with Taylor - my classmate from Walnut Creek."

"Anything?"

"Yes, they were good friends. Says Kaitlyn had an older boyfriend, Greg, and from Taylor's description there may be a few red flags. Is that in your notes?"

"Kaitlyn's parents said she wasn't seeing anyone, but they seemed a little strict with her. It wouldn't surprise me that a

GO WITH GRACE 89

teenage girl from a protective family would hide a boyfriend, certainly an older one. What red flags?"

"Controlling. Love bombing. Older."

Martina shook her head. "Did you get a last name?"

"No last name."

"I'll run it by the family to confirm and see what else I can find. We'll talk more in a few days when you're back in the office."

"Sure thing."

We said our goodbyes, and I headed to my car with thoughts of both Brendon and Dillon on my mind. Two men who both needed my help. And my help was exactly what they would get.

19

SELENA

I shoved my textbook into my backpack while I mentally ran through all of my to-do list items for the day. I picked up my backpack and slung it over my shoulder and headed out of the classroom. First item on my list was to fill my veins with as much caffeine as possible at the campus café. My mind and body were like jelly. Jelly brains didn't make for good investigations.

I reached the café, opened the door and inhaled the scent of fresh-roasted coffee beans. *Yes. Yes. Yes.* I stepped up to the counter, placed my order and then stepped aside to wait for my morning brew. I was scrolling through emails on my phone when I heard a familiar voice. "Fancy seeing you here."

"Oh, hi, Taylor. Sorry, didn't see you there." I stuffed my phone into my backpack.

"Getting a bit of a morning pick-me-up?"

Taylor was too perky. "Yeah, need lots of it today."

"I thought a lot about what we were talking about yesterday - you know about Kaitlyn? I had some questions. Do you have any time to talk?"

I eyed a cup being placed on the counter with my name on it. "Hold that thought." I approached the counter and picked up my steaming cup of coffee, taking a sip before securing a lid on top. I returned to Taylor. "I was on my way to the library if you want to walk and talk."

"Sure."

"Do you need to wait for your order?"

"I didn't order anything, I saw you come in and figured I'd come in and ask if you had a few minutes to talk about Kaitlyn."

Was that weird? I took another sip of my coffee and felt the initial drips of caffeine rushing to my veins. I opened my eyes wider. I really needed to get more sleep. I led the way out of the café and began heading toward the café.

"Have there been any developments in Kaitlyn's case? Have you found her yet?" Taylor asked.

We just talked yesterday. This was actual life, not the movies where crimes were solved within a thirty-minute window. "No new developments yet, but what you told me was helpful. Nobody had given a description of her boyfriend before."

"Really?"

"You're the only one who even knew about him. Not even her parents knew she was dating someone."

"Strange."

The fact that only Taylor knew about Greg could mean a couple of things. One, Kaitlyn had kept her relationship hidden because she was afraid of her parents' reaction or two, Taylor was making it up. I studied Taylor's face, which seemed to be a shade paler than before. She was either very concerned about her friend or filled with guilt that she hadn't shared the details about Greg earlier - or something worse.

We reached the library, and my sleep depravation had

caused me to temporarily forget my dreadful lunch date with Van. Now I needed a plan to stake out the library computers while avoiding the creepy librarian. Next time I'd wear a hat.

I led Taylor to a study table that was closest to the downstairs computers. I had a perfect view of all users and alerts set for when KT posted on her social media page. I sat down, pleased with my plan. I looked across the table at Taylor. "Are you okay?"

"I just can't help but wonder if I had said something about Greg earlier, would Kaitlyn be missing?"

Guilt. I knew the feeling well. "Maybe. Maybe not. Either way, if something bad happened to her, it's not your fault."

Taylor dropped down into her chair. "I hope she's okay." She glanced up at me. "Please let me know if I can help. I mean it."

I thought about that for a moment. How could Taylor help? "Do you remember what Greg looked like?"

She grimaced. "Yes. He was gross."

"Let me talk to my stepmom. It might be useful to have you sit down with a sketch artist. It could lead us to his identity and then maybe it could help us find it Kaitlyn. Is that something you'd be willing to do?"

"Absolutely."

A sparkle returned to Taylor's blue eyes. I knew it felt good to think you could help. Maybe Taylor wasn't so bad. I unpacked my schoolbooks and my laptop. They landed on the wood table with a thud. Oops. I noticed Taylor was sitting motionless, watching me. "Is there something else?"

"I had one more question for you. You said that you knew of a situation similar to Kaitlyn's - a girl dating a creepy guy. Were you talking about you?"

"Me and unfortunately, many others too. Why?"

"I have a date on Friday with an older guy and I don't want

to make a similar mistake. I don't have a lot of dating experience."

"Does he seem like someone who is controlling or violent?"

"I don't think so but..."

I smirked, understanding where she was going. "You never know. Yeah, that's a good point. I can forward you a website that lists all the red flags to look out for."

"Thanks. I mean, I don't think that this guy is bad or anything, but I don't know him very well either. It's actually Dillon from our economics class. You know him, what do you think?"

I stopped fiddling with my items and looked up at her. Dillon had a date with Taylor? Dillon was dating someone when he was being stalked? Why would he have not told me about this potentially major information? I mean, he could date whoever he wanted. It was just a little surprising that he was going out with Taylor - a freshman. "Dillon, he seems okay, I guess. I mean, I don't know him that well either."

"He seems great, I'm sure I'm overreacting, but this whole thing with Kaitlyn's got me thinking that every guy could be a potentially bad person, you know?"

"Oh, I know. It took me a long time after a terrible relationship to even consider dating again, but there are good guys out there."

"Are you dating anyone now?"

I shook my head and tried not to laugh at the silly idea. "Oh no, I haven't dated in quite some time."

"Really? Why? You're so pretty."

Not sure what pretty had to do with anything. *Youth.* "I haven't wanted to date, it's not a big deal."

"That's cool. I bet you get asked out all the time. Actually, I'm surprised you aren't dating Dillon."

Was she fishing? I wasn't interested in Dillon - at least not interested in dating Dillon or anyone. I eyed Taylor. "Not that surprising."

She shook her head. "Oh, I meant nothing by it. It's just that he's a good-looking guy. You seem really nice, attractive, and smart. It just seems like the two of you hit it off. I've seen you together a few times. You look friendly."

She'd seen us together a few times? I cocked my head, thinking about that.

She followed up with the quick, "After class, you know?"

After class? Was she being defensive? Had she realized she had slipped up? Taylor couldn't be his stalker, right? He was going on a date with her. Based on what I'd read about stalkers, it made little sense someone would stalk someone they were dating. It didn't fit the pattern. More likely someone who was stalking him had a grudge or secret affection. I brushed the ideas aside. "Well, whatever you thought, I assure you we're just friends."

Taylor didn't seem satisfied with the response, but it was all she was going to get out of me. The details of the KT investigation were private.

"Oh, okay."

I flipped open the lid of my laptop; I needed to study and to focus on the investigation. Discussing Taylor's romantic plans with Dillon were not a priority. I glanced over at Taylor, who was now pulling out her books to study as well. She was obviously a little intuitive and got the hint.

An hour later, Taylor packed up her things and said she had to run, but that it was nice talking earlier, and I'd see her in class. I waved as she left. Not a single hit on the KT's Facebook account. I wondered how long I'd have to wait before I got a lead.

Four hours later and I was nearly asleep but had gotten a lot of my homework done. No hits on KT's Facebook account. I assumed no emails to Dillon; he said he would text if he received any. No KT sighting, but the night wasn't a total bust. My homework was done, and that was something. Next item on my to-do list: sleep.

20

TAYLOR

I skipped to the Café with butterflies fluttering in my belly. I was going on a date with Dillon. At last, our story would begin. I'm glad it was all going in such a positive direction. I was beginning to like Selena, and I would hate to have to cause her any more grief. I opened the door and stepped in, inhaling the smell of coffee and sugar cookies. I surveyed the large and bustling café that seated fifty or so students studying, drinking coffee, eating giant cookies, and sandwiches. Some had soup. I spotted Dillon sitting by himself at a table for two.

I think the fact that he arrived early was a good sign. He obviously didn't want to be late and make a bad impression. *So sweet.* I approached with a spring in my step. He glanced up from his phone. "Oh, hi Taylor." His eyes sparkled at me like gorgeous blue diamonds.

"Have you ordered yet?" I asked.

"Not yet, I just got here."

I took a seat, draping my bag on the back of the chair. Within moments the server was at our table taking our order. I hadn't reviewed the menu, but it didn't matter. I'd seen enough when I'd walked in. We gave our order and then we were alone.

I stared into his eyes. "Thank you again for agreeing to be my study buddy. I think it will really help me. I don't know if my bad study habits for this class are because of how boring the subject is or if it's because there are too many distractions." He was definitely distracting me, but that wasn't the reason for my lackluster grades. I was an 'A' student. I had simply needed an 'in' with Dillon.

"No problem. I need to study too. Sometimes I slack off, especially on Fridays. You're keeping me on the straight and narrow."

He was adorable. "Great. Well, I'm happy to help."

"How was your week?"

He was asking me personal questions about my life. A very good sign. Sure, we'd declared it a study-buddy session, but I was definitely having first-date vibes. "Mostly good, but I received some weird news. News I'm still processing."

"Weird news?"

I explained to him about Kaitlyn and my conversation with Selena. "Oh, is that what Selena needed to talk to you about?"

I nodded. "Yeah, she wanted to know if I knew her. I told her everything I knew. I hadn't realized that she worked for a private investigation firm, did you?"

"Yep. I read it in the papers."

"In the papers?"

"Yes, it was all over the news and social media. It made her infamous around here for a while."

No wonder she didn't have any social media. "Oh, what happened?"

"Our sophomore year, she was investigating a case and her boyfriend was murdered by the people she was investigating."

My mouth dropped open, pretending to be hearing the news for the first time. "Seriously?"

"Yep." Dillon when on to describe the entire horrible story.

Although it wasn't extra information, hearing it aloud, it made me feel terrible about keying her car. Poor Selena. I should try to befriend her. She probably could use another friend. Gosh, what she must've gone through. No wonder she didn't date anymore. On the upside, that probably meant she really wasn't interested in Dillon. I tried to suppress my pleasure at the thought that Selena was probably the last person who may be a threat to my relationship with Dillon. This was glorious news. I really did like her. She seemed so strong and confident and capable. I'm glad I hadn't done anything too drastic.

"Wow."

"Yeah, she seems okay now. A little guarded, but can you blame her?" Dillon said.

"Seriously. When I met with her, she mentioned she was helping you with the class."

"You two talked about me?" Dillon asked.

"Oh, I just mentioned that I was meeting you today."

His smile had faded, and I wanted to know why. "Oh yeah, that. That's right, yeah, she's been really helpful." He hesitated, but then continued. "Did she say anything else about me?"

Why did he care what she thought of him? Was it that he had a crush on Selena, but she'd refused him because of her terrible past? I shook it off. He was here with me now. "No, nothing else. Why, were you two an item?"

"No, of course not. I just don't want her telling people that she's helping me with the class because I'm not doing well. I'm getting an A, I had lost my notes, and she helped me, that's all."

"Oh, I don't think she'd say anything bad about you. She said you seem okay."

He deflated.

I think Dillon really needed to focus on me and not Selena. "How was your week?"

The server returned with our order. For my Dillon, a sandwich and a bag of chips along with a large iced coffee. For me, a turkey sandwich, chips, and cola. I was hungry since I hadn't eaten all day because I'd been too nervous about our date. I popped open my bag of barbecue potato chips and crunched down. Yummy. I watched him as he took a bite before telling me about his week. I wanted him to know I was a superb listener and would be a great girlfriend. "I've been so swamped with work, school, and studying for the LSAT. Graduation will be here before I know it."

"I didn't realize you work. What do you do?"

"I work at a law firm, part time. I help with filing and administrative tasks. Nothing fancy, just something to get in the door of a law office."

"Do you need to take economics to be a lawyer?"

"No, I'm majoring in psychology and minoring in business. That's why I'm taking econ as a senior." He continued to tell me about his career ambitions as an entertainment lawyer.

"That's so cool. I mean, I'm a business major, but I'm minoring in theater. I wanted to major in theater, but my parents wouldn't go for it. A business major was the only way they'd agree to pay for college. My genuine passion is acting. I love movies and TV. I think it's so cool you want to go into the entertainment industry too. I'm not exactly sure what I'll do yet, but I know it will be in front of an audience." We were so perfect for each other. It was as if fate brought us together that day at the volunteer fair. I knew it then. I knew it now.

We would have the most amazing life. He'd move out to Los Angeles, I'd follow behind, maybe change schools. We'd both focus on our careers before getting married. We'd have the most beautiful house in the Hollywood Hills.

He said, "I hadn't realized that. I have an uncle who is in the industry. He is the one who told me about all the different jobs there are in entertainment - one thing he mentioned was the need for good lawyers. I'm a big movie buff myself so I thought hey, I love the law and the entertainment industry, so it was a perfect fit. I could really help people - like new actors just getting into the business. My job would be to make sure the talent didn't get swindled into signing terrible contracts. It happens too often to young stars."

I nodded furiously. "Yes, there's so many horror stories about how managers and agents practically steal from their clients. It's so awesome that you want to be an advocate for them." He was so awesome. My guy, a humanitarian.

He continued to ask about my own ambitions, and we chatted away. He listened to my dreams of becoming a dramatic actress, taking important roles that meant something. I'd tell a story with a message. I couldn't wait to accept my first acting award and thank Dillon in my speech. I didn't tell him that part; I wanted it to be a surprise.

We finished up our lunch, and Dillon pulled out his textbook. "I suppose we should hit the books." He smiled.

I melted.

I suppose studying was part of the deal. It would be difficult to focus on economics, with him sitting across from me. My body was vibrating with joy. This couldn't have gone any better.

I caved and started in on my homework. I didn't want him to think this entire thing was a ruse, even though it had been. It had been painful to have to miss so many questions on my exam just to appear as if I needed a tutor. I hadn't told him I was actually the valedictorian of my high school, choosing San Francisco University for its stellar theater program. I didn't need a tutor, but I needed Dillon.

After finishing the first homework set, I decided to call it quits and hoped Dillon would suggest another activity for us, one more fun and romantic. I shut my book. "All done."

"Wow, you're fast. How did you do?" He leaned over and reviewed at my answers. "Wow, looks like they're all correct. You must have been right, all you needed was a study buddy." He quipped.

"All I needed was you." I said with a smile. "How about you? Are you finished?"

"With econ, yes. This was fun."

"It was." I packed up my things into my bag and he stood up, but left his things in place.

"Are you staying?"

He said, "I still have some other things to do. But I'll see you next week okay?"

"Oh, okay. Well, bye." I exited the café, wondering why he hadn't made another date with me. But I shook it off. He was so busy he needed to do his homework. It was understandable, although it was a Friday night. It was probably nothing, and I didn't want to thwart his ambitious efforts to get all his homework done. We had the rest of our lives to chat, watch movies, hold hands, kiss, and take part in other naughty things. No rush needed. I didn't even feel the cold air touch my skin as I floated home with a wide grin spread across my face.

A FEW HOURS LATER, A RUMBLE ERUPTED IN MY TUMMY. I could definitely go for another sandwich and chips to relive those moments sitting across from Dillon. I'd order it to go. A dinner for one, but a memory of two. And who knows, maybe he's still at the café burning the midnight oil? A chance encounter. He'd ask if I'd like to join him, of course. I'd pretend like I didn't want to bother him, but I would join him.

We'd talk, and we'd laugh. He'd invite me to his apartment, or I'd invite him to go back to my dorm. We'd watch a movie and then transition our relationship to a physical one. The butterflies returned as I hurried down to the café.

I stepped inside and froze. There he sat in the same spot, but he wasn't alone. They were both packing up and heading straight for me.

Fury raced through my body. I quickly stepped back outside and hurried out to the right and peered around the corner. They laughed as he opened the door to the outside. He had his hand on her back as he ushered her out of the restaurant. I rushed down to the corner to remain out of sight. She swore she didn't date. She'd had a sad story. Yet, there she was with my Dillon on a Friday night laughing, not studying. Why were they both lying to me? My heart nearly pounded out of my chest.

That was it. I liked Selena, but I loved Dillon and only one of us could have him. I was that one. All is fair in love and war. Sorry, Selena, but you can't mess with my destiny.

21

SELENA

I STOOD UP FROM THE TABLE AND GROANED. A LAUGH FELL out of Dee's mouth. "A little sore?"

I was beyond sore. My insides were screaming and my muscles were begging me to stop the torture. "A little."

"You did great today."

"I definitely feel like I deserved those waffles."

Dee smiled. "It's good to see you eating carbs."

"At heart, I will always be a sugar fiend." But at this point in my life, I'd only allow myself to indulge in sweets after I had pushed my body to its limits in the gym. I smiled. "Sometimes I wonder if it's the only reason I hit the gym." We both laughed as we exited the restaurant.

Dee and I had decided that we would do a weekly brunch after our Krav Maga class. Sometimes the promise of waffles was the only thing that got me through the class. Waffles aside, it felt good to be pushing my body to its limits once again. I'd only been back for a week, but I could already feel my body getting stronger, despite its screams for me to stop. It felt like life was getting back to normal, at least my normal. Not normal-people normal. Selena normal. Investigating. Excelling at school. Getting fit. Becoming lethal.

I was only a few short months from being able to devote all my time to helping other people and being the best person I could be.

We approached the parking lot and stopped in between our cars. She said, "This was great. When should we meet up to do our weekly shooting range date?"

It was ironic that I had once helped Dee recover from a life-changing attack, now here she was pulling me back from my own life-changing event. She was sneaky. She'd convinced me to do two activities and meals out a week. I wonder if she was in cahoots with Martina. Either way, I was grateful. I was lucky to have a friend who could see past my tough exterior and offer a lifeline when I needed it. "Any night this week would be fine. I can shuffle other responsibilities, how about you?"

A smile tugged at Dee's lips. "Well, actually I can't on Friday but any other day. Not Friday."

I hadn't seen Dee quite this coy in, well... forever. I can't believe I didn't notice it before. Her aqua blue eyes had a twinkle I hadn't seen in a long while. She'd always been a positive force. She was usually optimistic, strong, and smart, but something was different. It wasn't a 'I counseled my first survivor today' kind of sparkle. It was different. *It can't be.* "What is happening on Friday?"

Her eyes were bright and beautiful. "I have a date."

It is. "What? And you're just now mentioning it? We sat through waffles and whipped cream. Two cups of coffee. This is huge. Tell me everything." I beamed at her as I leaned back on my driver's side door. My heart was full as I listened to Dee describe the man she'd met and agreed to go on a date with. She was clearly smitten with him. I wonder what changed her mind about dating. Two years ago, she'd sworn off men after she'd been assaulted at the fraternity house. I'd always hoped that she would learn to trust men again, but she hadn't until now. I grinned. "I'm so happy for you. What changed? I know you haven't been interested in dating for a while."

She shook her head with a silly grin on her face. "I don't know. There's something about him. He's smart, handsome, and successful. He's actually... don't laugh."

I dragged my pointer finger across my chest. "Cross my heart."

"He's a police officer."

"What?"

"Yeah, we met at the self-defense class that I teach. He came in to do a demonstration and then we got to talking. Talking turned into coffee and then lunch and then at the end of lunch he asked me out to dinner."

"Wow. I know it's sappy, but I'm so happy for you. Oh, how things have changed over the years." I commented.

"Yeah, it just goes to show you that anything's possible. If I could find a guy that I'm willing to go on a date with, I think there is hope for all of us."

It was as if her voice was speaking into my soul, telling me I needed to move on. I needed to date again, or at least be open to the possibility. She got my butt back into the gym and had me on a new target-practice routine, but if she could convince me to date, she was a darn right miracle worker. Who knows, maybe she was. "Even the most hopeless may have hope."

Dee's head flew back as she laughed. "Did I detect a hint that maybe there's someone on your mind?"

"No, no. I'm saying maybe one day, but not today."

"Okay, but I've got my eye on you, missy."

"All right, I've got tons of stuff to do." I embraced her in a hug and we said our goodbyes.

I turned around to open my car door. It was already

unlocked. I mumbled, "What the heck?" When I opened the door, I saw it and froze. A folded note was sitting on my driver's seat. It hadn't been there when we entered the restaurant. I turned around and called out. "Hey, Dee, do you have any gloves?"

"I have a pair in my car. Give me a sec."

She returned with gloves. "What is it?"

"Someone left a note inside my car."

Worry crossed Dee's face as she handed me the gloves. I put them on and opened up the note. Rage filled my center. I showed the note to Dee, and she gasped. "Do you think it's the traffickers?"

I took the note back, and in that moment I knew the gloves weren't necessary. KT didn't leave prints. Voice shaking, I read it aloud. "If I see you with Dillon again, he'll end up like your last boyfriend, Brendon. Stay away from Dillon. This is your last warning." KT had officially crossed my fucking line. "This isn't from the traffickers. This is from KT. I have no doubt."

Dee's eyes were wide. "That is a death threat. KT is escalating. Whoever KT is, in my opinion, is someone with serious mental health issues. Maybe you should stay with me or your dad and Martina's until you find out KT's identity. This worries me."

That may be so, but now KT had more than a mental health issue to deal with. She had to deal with me. I would find KT and she would pay for everything she'd done to Dillon and to me. She would be locked up and justice would be served. KT didn't know who she was messing with. If KT was smart, she would know to run and hide because I was coming for her.

22

TAYLOR

I watched her from across the street. No tears this time. Just arms waving around. Good. I really didn't want to hurt her, even though she'd hurt me. I wasn't petty like that. But then again, maybe Selena needed to learn a lesson. I'd thought she was a stand-up person. A woman to admire, but no. She'd been a liar. She betrayed another woman. *Me.* I really didn't want to take drastic measures, so I truly hoped Selena now understood the seriousness of the situation. It was serious.

I recalled the previous evening when I'd drafted the note after I'd seen them together. After running back to my dorm, I'd rushed into the bathroom and screamed into a towel before pulling out the razor. I sat on the bathroom floor as I planned my next move. My revenge. My path back to Dillon. How the hell was he going to focus on me when that stupid Selena was around? Based on my research of the little investigator girl, she seemed to have a bit of a martyr complex. I suppose I should've researched her more thoroughly. I now understood threatening her did nothing. She thought she was invincible. But threaten someone she cared about and bingo. Hit her where it hurts.

Through my anger and heartache, tears had streaked down my face as I crafted the wording. I could barely see the words on the screen. After I'd calmed down and cleaned myself up, I pulled out the stationary that my ridiculous mother had given me as a high school graduation gift. She'd said it was for keeping in touch with my classmates. Seriously? Nobody wrote notes. Hello. Social media. Mom was living in the freaking dark ages. Although notes written with my left hand was a brilliant cover. I mean, really, who leaves a note these days? It would never get back to me. Maybe Mom wasn't so terrible. No, she was. She'd tried to control me for as long as I could remember. No more. Now, I was in control of my destiny, and my destiny included Dillon. I loved him. Had Selena loved Brendon like that? I bet that really got her that I knew his name. That's right, bitch, I'm on to you.

I continued to watch for her to call the police again. Like they could do anything. Useless. All I, or anyone, needed to do to get into Selena's old car was to watch a YouTube video or two and voila. Breaking in was easy as pie. Apple pie. And it was freezing outside. A young female wearing gloves didn't warrant a second glance. The cops wouldn't find anything. My phone buzzed, and I jumped. Geez, Taylor, calm down. Maybe it was Dillon. I checked the screen. Ugh. Mom again. Reject. I returned my focus to Selena and her pal, Dee. Yes, I'd read about Dee too. Two little commandos. Sure, they shot guns and they could kill you with their bare hands or whatever, but I had something they didn't. I had the element of invisibility. I had smarts. They wouldn't find me unless I wanted them to. Hmm. They both returned to their cars.

I ducked down and watched the time on my phone for five minutes, when I was fairly certain they'd be gone. During that time, I thought about what I'd do next, assuming Selena stayed away from Dillon.

I eased myself up to a sitting position. Both were gone. Now it was time for my next move. Game on, Selena.

23

SELENA

I stormed through the offices of Drakos Monroe Security & Investigations. I couldn't remember the last time I was this enraged. No wait, I could. It was when I found out that Ocampo had killed Brendon. The passionate fury inside of me had dimmed over the last eighteen months, but it was now reignited by the note on my driver's seat. This KT didn't know who she was messing with. Unlucky for KT, I was about to enlighten her on the error of her ways.

I threw my backpack down on the carpet a little harder than I should have. I needed to calm down. I needed to be able to talk this through with Martina in a rational manner. I needed to center myself. I counted backwards from ten, followed by breathing exercises. I shut my eyes and placed my hands on my thighs, counted and began. In and out. In and out. My plan had been to continue until I no longer wanted to run to the shooting range, remove my gun from the locker, and go on a shooting spree.

My meditation was disturbed when I heard footsteps heading my way. I flipped my eyelids open to find Martina watching me with her brow wrinkled. "Hi there. Is everything okay?"

I shook my head back and forth. "No, not okay." I explained the break-in to my car and about the note.

"I'm so sorry that happened and I agree with you, I don't think it was anyone related to the trafficking case. Have you made a police report?"

"Not yet. I wanted to get your take on the note. Am I overreacting to think it's a death threat?"

Martina shook her head. "No, I don't think you're overreacting. You should make a police report. The note and break-in are strong evidence that this KT person needs to be put away before they hurt someone."

"Okay, I'll call Officer Heller to let him know I've got another report to make."

"And if he doesn't come by or follow through, we know who we can bring this to." Martina added.

Friends in high places. Not a bad thing to have. "Lieutenant Tippin."

"Exactly."

"Are you going to be okay? Is there something else bothering you?"

I shrugged. "It's all of this KT business and the potential break in the trafficking case. All the memories are flying back fast and furious. There was something about the note that seemed to push me over the edge."

Did it make me weak that I couldn't let this go? Most of the time, I was ready for the fight, but sometimes I wished I could hide under a rock and live out my days pretending nothing bad had ever happened. But that wasn't my fate. I was a fighter and I wouldn't give up.

"Why don't we grab some tea and we can talk while we wait for the police to arrive?"

I nodded.

"I'll meet you in conference room one after you call Heller."

"Okay, thanks."

I ended the call with Officer Heller and headed toward the conference room. Martina was in the corner removing her tea bag from the mug before dropping it into the trash. I sat at the table in front of the mug of tea she'd placed there for me. I grabbed the mug by the handle and inhaled the peppermint several times before taking a sip of the hot beverage. It made me feel better, more calm at least. I set the mug back down on the table. "Thank you, Martina."

"No problem. What do you plan to do to find out who KT is?"

I still wanted to stake out the library. I felt like it was the best bet, but I needed to get more creative. "I've been considering how to more efficiently stake out the library. Sitting and waiting is time-consuming, although, I am ahead on my homework. I've been investigating the legality of placing cameras so that I can watch from afar and then pinpoint the location of KT when they post on social media or send Dillon an email."

The library was a public place; the legality was a gray area. I watched Martina and could practically see the hamster running around the wheel. "What are you thinking?" I asked Martina.

Would Martina approve? I hoped she would, because deceiving Martina was not a simple task. As it stood, I wondered how much she knew about my activity at Drakos Monroe regarding the trafficking case. Had I covered my tracks as well as I'd thought? Were they monitoring my every keystroke? If so, she hadn't mentioned it.

Martina folded her arms across her chest. "That would be risky. You could get in trouble for it. But on the other hand, it's sort of public place."

"My thoughts exactly."

"It's still risky, you understand that, right?"

"I wouldn't be using it in a court of law, I just need to know KT's identity and then we'd go from there."

I had a feeling Martina wouldn't be into the idea, she'd never been fond of my secret cameras in the past. To be fair, I'd had issues in the past after nearly being caught. This was different though, it was a public-ish place.

"When I say risky, I mean to you and your future - not a court case. Think about it this way. You plan to start your own firm. Is this something you would do for a paid client? Would you be willing to risk your own private investigator's license and your livelihood? Right now, at most you'd get a slap on the wrist or a misdemeanor charge. Which is fine, but you need to start to think about this as your own company. You lose your license, you lose your company. You need to ask yourself if continuing to take these types of risks is worth it?"

Damn. Martina had a point; one I hadn't even considered. I'd need to think about that after I had my PI license. But for now, I didn't have a license. I also don't think I'd get caught or even need the cameras up for very long. Even if I did, I could try to sweet-talk Van. *Ick.* The things I'd do for an investigation. As far as I was considered, the current risk was pretty low.

I took another sip of the peppermint tea before setting the cup back down on the table. "Okay, I think I know what I'm going to do."

Martina raised her hand in protest. "Don't tell me. I don't want to know." She winked and gave me a halfhearted smile. Martina knew exactly what I was going to do, but just in case, it was better she didn't have explicit knowledge of my plans.

"Now that that's settled, is there any news on Kaitlyn's case?"

Martina shifted in her chair and then flipped the lid open on her laptop. "Actually, I'm glad you brought it up. We've reviewed all the police reports and re-interviewed the family. Nobody had mentioned or heard of Greg, but the family confirmed Taylor March was her best friend for a long time, but they'd seen less of her recently. So, if anyone knew about a secret boyfriend, it would be Taylor. And if Taylor's intuition is correct, we need to find Greg. He could be the key to finding Kaitlyn."

My mood lifted. "So, Taylor could actually help find Kaitlyn. That's great news. I've already asked Taylor if she remembers what he looks like and she said she'd be willing to sit with a sketch artist."

"Excellent idea. Can you reach out to Taylor to see if she could come in this week? The sooner the better."

"Will do. I'll text her." I paused as I wondered if I should get Martina's opinion on Dillon dating Taylor. Maybe it wasn't strange? "Another thing... Taylor and I were talking at the library the other day and she mentioned she had a date with Dillon. I haven't asked Dillon about it yet, but do you think it's strange that Dillon would date someone when he's being stalked?"

Martina sat expressionless. It was as if she could read everybody's facial expressions and moods and nuances, but nobody could read hers. At least she was thinking, which meant she must've thought it was a bit weird. "It's a little odd, but he is a young man. Is Taylor pretty?"

I smirked. *Men.* "She is. Tall, blonde, you know — the total package."

"Is it strange? Maybe. I mean, he should refrain for Taylor's sake. She could become a target herself. Look how KT has focused on you and you're not even dating this guy. Imagine if it was a real love interest? What if the stalker reaches out to Taylor? She could be in danger."

Double damn. I hadn't even thought of that. Taylor could be in danger. Should I tell her to keep an eye out for people following her? But what if Dillon doesn't want her to know that he has a stalker? "That's a good point. I'll call Dillon tonight and ask him about Taylor, if for no other reason to make sure Taylor is safe. But if she gets notes and threats, it wouldn't be fair to Taylor to not let her know the risks and the dangers of dating Dillon."

My heart was a bit heavy thinking of Dillon dating some-body else. Not that we were an item or would be. We were going different directions in a few short months. I was gradu-ating and starting my own PI firm. He would eventually head off to law school to who knows where. Why did I keep having to remind myself he was a client and that it would never work?

"Good plan."

At least Martina approved of some of my activities. My phone buzzed, and I picked up. "Selena Bailey."

"This is Officer Heller, I'm at the front entrance of the building."

"I'll be right down."

I quickly explained to Martina that Heller had arrived before strutting out of the conference room. The past two weeks had been a whirlwind, yet just a few weeks before that, my life was pretty boring. I was reviewing records, secretly investigating my boyfriend's killers, and attending classes. Now I was involved in two different investigations, attending classes, and planning to start my own PI firm. Life was exciting once again. The only question was, was that a good thing?

24

SELENA

I jogged toward the building to meet Dillon. By the time I arrived at the entrance, my ears ached from the cold. I should've just told him the latest update over the phone. It was early and freezing, two of my least favorite things, but I had already texted him last night asking him to meet me before class. I wanted to talk to him in person so I could gauge his reaction. It was strictly business - not personal.

I opened the door and spotted him right inside. He stood there with a sheepish grin and two matching paper coffee cups in each hand. "Hey."

"Hey. I brought you coffee. It's a latte, I remembered that's what you ordered at our last meeting, I hope it's okay."

I shook off the fact he knew my drink order. It was no big deal. So, he had a good memory. "Thanks. I definitely could use the caffeine."

"Should we go somewhere more private?"

Not a bad idea in case KT was lurking. "Sure, you think there's anyone in the classroom yet?" Unlikely.

"I haven't checked."

"I'll look, stay here."

I approached the door to the classroom and opened it. I stepped in and surveyed the empty auditorium. I turned around and waved him over.

Dillon nodded and followed me inside.

We seated ourselves in the row closest to the door. I faced him. "Okay, I wanted to give you the latest. There's no easy way to say this, so I'll just come out with it." I explained the threatening note.

He looked stricken. Pale, even. "Are you okay?" I asked him.

"I guess. I knew KT was becoming unhinged and feared it could get ugly, but now that she's actually threatening my life, it's really hitting home." He shook his head back and forth. "Are you sure it was from KT?"

"I'm not 100% certain, but the people who killed Brendon had a very direct approach - there was nothing anonymous about it. Trust me." I said with as little emotion as I could muster. I didn't need to fall apart now.

He let out a breath. "Okay, so what do we do now?"

"KT still thinks I'm a romantic possibility for you and appears to be watching us, so we don't provoke her we should try avoid being seen together. Also, I've been working on staking out the library. Hopefully, in a few days, we'll know the identity of KT and we can put an end to all of this."

"Is that it?"

"Not exactly." This was going to be harder than I thought. I watched as he checked his phone, shook his head and put the phone back in his pocket. "Was that KT again?"

"No, actually it's someone else. What were you saying?"

I took a sip of my latte. "I was with Taylor last week and she mentioned you had a date. Are you dating her?"

His cheeks turned pink. "No. I mean, kind of. We met up to study and had lunch. I got the vibe she thought it was more, but she's just too young. She keeps texting me, clearly not getting the hint that I'm not interested."

"Why don't you just tell her that?"

"I don't want to hurt her feelings."

Didn't want to hurt her feelings? Ugh. What did he think that ghosting her felt like, a bunch of roses? Why did people do that?

I stepped back. Maybe Dillon wasn't the guy I thought he was. I thought he was a good, upstanding guy. This ghosting technique was probably why somebody was stalking him. It was probably some poor girl he didn't even remember that he'd went out with. At least Taylor was safe. "Is this something that you do often?" I said a bit harsher than I probably should have.

His eyes widened. "What do you mean?"

"Do you go out with girls and then just completely ghost them?"

"No, I mean, not always. I don't actually go out with that many girls. Taylor's nice and she's cute, but she's too young and not my type."

"But you've done this type of thing before? This could be how this whole KT thing started. You know, it doesn't feel very good to go out with someone and then they just don't return your calls. For the record, it's mean, and it hurts. So if you're trying to spare Taylor's feelings, you're failing."

"I guess I've never thought of it that way. I'll talk to her."

"Good. But so you know, it may not be a good idea to date anyone until the KT situation is resolved. Anyone you date will probably become a target. So, if you can handle not dating right now, it's for the best."

"That's a good point. Okay, I won't date anyone until this is over. Thank you."

I relaxed. "Now we have that cleared up, we should split up. You never know, KT could be in this class."

"You think so?"

"It could be anyone, we have to be smart."

"Okay. Talk to you later." He stood up to take another seat when the door to the classroom creaked open.

We both turned.

"Oh, hi, Taylor."

Her mouth dropped open. "Oh, hi, Selena. Hi, Dillon."

"Hey, Taylor." Dillon said as he continued to the aisle. "You're early."

"Trying to get the worm." She chuckled without sincerity. I wonder if she was worried that I was sitting with Dillon. She clearly liked him. I could practically feel her pain. "We were just comparing notes from class last week."

Dillon nodded. "Yeah, I was just heading over to a seat closer to the front. You want to join me?"

It wasn't a move I would've recommended because now it seemed like he was leading the poor girl on. It would only make the blow even harder when Dillon told her he wasn't interested in dating her. There really ought to be a dating manual that is distributed to middle school students.

She smiled at Dillon before saying, "Sure. See you later, Selena," without turning to look at me.

I shook my head. After Dillon had 'the talk' with her, I'd reach out to see if she was okay. I'm sure Taylor would be all right, eventually.

25

DILLON

I SAT DOWN AND WATCHED AS TAYLOR TOOK THE SEAT NEXT to me. She was sweet and cute, but I couldn't get Selena out of my head. Maybe I could tell Taylor about KT and explain that we couldn't date because of KT - for her own safety. As it was, my safety was in question. Was Selena right? Was KT some girl I had actually gone on a date with and then never talked to again?

Well, I certainly wouldn't do that again. I needed to end this KT business so I could move on with my life. I hoped moving on included Selena. My thoughts of her were interrupted. "So, how was your weekend? Were you super busy with school and work?"

I nodded and looked into her pleading eyes. I wasn't so dense that I didn't realize she was probably trying to figure out why I hadn't texted her back. "Yes, it was a mostly homework and LSAT prep kinda weekend. How about you?"

Taylor fidgeted in her seat. "It was good. I accomplished a lot too. I think I was inspired by our study session - maybe we can have another on Wednesday?"

Would that be a good time to have the talk with her? Well, it would either be then or before then. Until the talk, I'd remain friendly. "That works for me. Same place?"

She nodded with a glimmer of hope. "Great. Maybe I'll try one of their cookies this time."

"Sounds like a plan." I forced a smile, and she asked if I'd seen any new movies lately and then described some of her favorites. We chatted until the professor arrived and the class began. She was so optimistic and full of energy it would be difficult to let her down. For now, maybe I'd give her the KT safety excuse as to why I couldn't date her. It should at least hold her off for a while until I could tell her the whole truth, if needed. Maybe she'd figure out on her own we weren't a suitable match. Wouldn't that be something? I deserved something to go easy for a change, didn't I?

26

TAYLOR

I HAD DECIDED TO ARRIVE TO CLASS EARLY, HOPING TO SEE Dillon. A casual bumping into. Our eyes would meet and he'd apologize for his lack of messages. We'd make another date. Our story would continue.

I had been certain Selena was smart enough to stay away from him. Clearly, I was wrong about that. My heart nearly stopped when I saw the two of them engaged in conversation. I almost ran out in tears, but sucked it up. It required every bit of courage I had in myself to put on a happy face and act as if all was well. When in reality, I wanted to scream and shout. I wanted to pull out Selena's hair and stab her in the chest. I pictured blood dripping down her front as I faked a smile and greeted them.

It worked. For now. He left her to sit with me. To talk to me. Maybe I should leave Selena alone? Maybe she was just helping him with his class notes? If that were true then why the sneakiness? My heart ached at what I knew was the truth. He was attracted to her, but I also knew he liked me. Once she was out of the picture for good, I would have all his attention. The semester was only three more months, I could simply let her fade away as she graduates and then I'd have him all to myself. Or I could take more drastic measures. No reason for a decision now.

Now I needed to figure out the perfect plan to get Dillon to fall in love with me. If I achieved that with no more stunts, all was well that ended well. I needed to be smart.

A jingle in the lock forced me to turn toward the front door. In stepped, Mandy. She gave a bright smile. "Hi Tay."

"Hey."

"Not studying at the library today?"

I shook my head. "I was there earlier. I wanted a snack, so I came home to finish up my homework. How was the rally?" Mandy was always taking part in whatever protest was on campus. God bless her. Somebody had to fight the good fight. She was a freshman, like me, but she seemed more worldly somehow. Mandy had even been on a few dates since the semester had started.

"It was pretty good. A news team showed up so that should help bring awareness to the cause."

"That's great." I said with as much enthusiasm as I could fake. I started to ask her a question, but hesitated.

Mandy set down her bag on the ground and joined me on the sofa. "What is it?"

I swiveled to face her. "Can I ask you about something?"

"Of course."

"So, there's this guy."

Mandy's brown eyes brightened. "Ooh. Tell me more."

"We've gone out for a study date and I want to move from the study-buddy zone to the relationship zone. We have another study date on Wednesday. Any tips?"

Mandy hopped off the couch. "Yes. I have just the thing." She rushed into our bedroom and returned with a dress in hand. She held up a low-cut black sweater dress I'd seen her wear before. It was sexy. "You have to get him thinking about sex. A subtly revealing dress is just the thing. Pair it with some tights and boots and you're fall-appropriate while still looking stunning. With your figure you'll knock his socks off."

I eyed the dress. "I can borrow it?"

"Heck yeah. Now give me all the details. I want to hear all about him."

I grinned as told her all about Dillon. It was nice to finally have someone to talk to about him. I hadn't made many - or any - friends since I started college, Mandy was basically it. At times, she was a little too political for me, but she was nice and easy to talk to. Not a bad first roommate. If she wasn't such a slob, she'd be perfect.

We continued to plot how I'd get Dillon to fall head over heals for me. I had been uneasy about seeing him with Selena again, but now I was feeling on top of the world. It would all work out just as I imagined.

27

SELENA

I PRESSED IGNORE ON THE INCOMING CALL FROM DILLON and started my car. I couldn't deal with him right now because I had bigger fish to fry.

My heart raced as I backed out of the parking lot. I prayed I would arrive at the house in Millbrae in time to watch the show. It was a twenty-minute drive from campus, but I was determined to make it in fifteen. I needed to be there. I needed to see his face - whoever he was. I also wanted him to see my face and know that I hadn't faded into oblivion. I was still around and I was still going to take him down. There was no handling me.

I sped along the highway as thoughts raced around my mind. For eighteen months I'd been waiting for this - a break in the trafficking case. A break in the investigation into Brendon's murder.

My body was vibrating as I listened to Detective Brown explain they were making an arrest today at a house in Millbrae. The man they were arresting was suspected of being Ocampo's boss, maybe even the leader of the entire Bay Area trafficking ring. Brown gave me an address, but not a name. I was unsure if that was intentional or not.

I was partially in disbelief that the investigation into the traffickers was coming to an end. Was it possible the traffickers would finally pay for what they did to Brendon, those women, girls, and God knows who else? I knew I could never get every trafficking cell in the world, but I had planned to get the one who hurt Brendon. I only wish it had been me who discovered the creep's identity and address. My justice would look a little different from the police's.

The thought that my journey was ending was surreal. It had been my driving force for so long. It was why I pushed ahead to graduate early and to follow Martina's rules so that I could get my PI license. It kept me going when all I wanted to do was give up and crawl into a cave and spend my days dining on sandwiches and canned soup. I didn't feel that I was worthy of being around the rest of the world, but I knew I owed it to Brendon to bring his killers to justice. It kept me from going to that dark place in my mind and into that cave.

After Brendon's funeral, Martina and my dad had sat me down and told me it wasn't my fault and that Ocampo was to blame. I remember the moment like it was yesterday.

WE WERE SITTING AT THE DINING TABLE AT MY DAD AND Martina's house. My face was streaked with tears and I stared blankly at the wall. Dad sat on my right, Martina on the left. My father had a pained look on his face as he spoke. "Selena, we're here for you, anything you need. I love you. I'm so glad that you are in my life. I feel grateful that you weren't hurt and that you will continue with us in this lifetime. We missed so many years together. My heart would shatter if something were to happen to you. I'm so proud of the young woman you've become. How you fight for the justice of people who need someone to fight for them. I'm proud that you're excelling in your studies at San Francisco University. Something I never did. Nobody in our family ever did. You will be the first graduate in our family and I could not be more proud. Please don't blame yourself for this. You're doing what any good person would do because that's who you are, Selena. You fight for the little guy. This is just one time you didn't win."

I had heard the words, but I didn't watch his face after he had begun speaking. I couldn't bear to see the pain in his eyes that he could've lost me too. Martina had been quiet. Dad didn't blame me for Brendon's death, but Martina must know that I was partially to blame. I glanced back at my dad with fresh tears streaming. "Thanks Dad, but I'll be fine." I watched as he exchanged glances with Martina. They didn't think I'd be fine, but I knew I would. It wasn't my first trip to devastation. Even at the young age of twenty, I'd already discovered my mother's dead body and had been held captive and nearly killed. I could handle this because I knew in my heart that I would get justice for Brendon. I had wiped the tears with the back of my hand and shifted my attention to Martina. "Will they find who did this?"

She shrugged. "I don't know, honey. They may, or they may never."

Martina wasn't one to mince words.

I stared into her eyes. "I think they will be brought to justice."

She shut her eyes as if she were trying to shut out my thoughts. Martina must know I wouldn't let it go. Not ever.

I picked at the piece of lint on my sweater and watched the motion as if it were the only thing happening in the room. I pretended to believe the pep talk would make a difference. It wouldn't. I'd already learned the lesson. Life wasn't easy, and it sure as heck wasn't fair.

My therapist always told me we can't control what other people do, we can only control how we react to them. I can only control my own behavior, my own thoughts, and my own actions. And control them is what I would do. That action would be to find Ocampo's boss. The one who gave the order to kill Brendon. I looked back up at Martina with determination in my eyes. "Will Drakos Monroe investigate?"

She shook her head back and forth. "No, it's an open police investigation. We don't get involved unless the case has gone cold. It's better to let the police handle this and you should let the police handle it."

My eyes narrowed and thought of how I could convince her otherwise. "But we could still look into the connections. We already have more information than the police."

Ever stoic, she responded. "No, we will not do that. It's far too dangerous to continue to look into the traffickers. We need to and we will let the police handle it."

That didn't sit well with me. The police were supposed to have handled finding Penny David when the five-year-old had gone missing, and when Emily Harrington, another little girl, had also gone missing a few months later. They failed to find either of them. I found them. There was no way I was going to leave the task of finding Brendon's killer to the police.

As I reached the exit, it occurred to me that, once again, Martina had been right, and I'd been wrong. I really hated that. The police had found them and I hadn't. It was bittersweet, but exciting at the same time.

I turned down the street. I hadn't needed the exact address. Buzzing overhead were a couple of black helicopters and a dozen cop cars parked outside one very large residence. I looked around the neighborhood that was filled with luxury vehicles and neighbors standing outside, likely wondering what was happening in their perfect neighborhood. I parked my car and began walking toward the house. A uniformed officer, that I didn't recognize, held up his hand to stop me. "Ma'am, you can't come any closer."

Ma'am? I was twenty-one and didn't look a day over sixteen. "I'm with Detective Brown. Please let him know I'm here."

He demanded identification before radioing it in. No trust. Had this been two years ago, I would've ignored the barricade and the officer's order and marched on, but I didn't want to do anything to mess up the arrest.

I watched as the front door of the home opened and Detective Brown stepped out and jogged toward me. "Selena, you made it."

"Yes, where is he?"

"He's inside - handcuffed. They're questioning him as the other officers are searching his home. They're not getting much from him at this point since he asked for his lawyer. I don't recommend you speak to him, but I wanted you to be here for this. We kept him here until your arrival."

I studied the man who had accomplished what I couldn't. "Thank you."

"We're going to take him down to the station, it's probably best to stay here, but you can watch as we put him into the back of a black-and-white."

I nodded as my heart nearly beat out of my chest. I wanted to rush into the house and attack the person. A person whose name I didn't even know. The detective motioned to one officer. "Tell him it's okay to bring him out."

The officer said, "Yes, sir," before hurrying off.

Detective Brown turned away. "I'll stay with you. We can watch together."

I grabbed Detective Brown's arm as I saw the man in cuffs led out of the house and toward a police vehicle. He had tan skin, dark hair and a nose like a pig with a round belly to match. I was flooded with emotion. I wanted to scream. I wanted to cry. That sad excuse for a man had consumed my life for eighteen months. He reached the car, ten feet away from where we stood. The pig man turned and our eyes met. He smirked before he was tucked gingerly into the back of the car. In that moment, my rage returned in full force. If he thought he was getting away with this, he was wrong - one way or another he'd get his just desserts.

28

SELENA

AFTER AN EMOTIONAL NIGHT, I SCROLLED THROUGH MY phone as I sunk into my sofa. Another post from KT on Facebook. 'Feeling like the luckiest girl in the Universe to have such a wonderful guy in my life' with an illustration of two red hearts attached. *Yikes*. I had my faults, but being delusional wasn't one of them - well, not usually. Speaking of 'such a wonderful guy' I needed to call Dillon back. I hope nothing worse than a social media post had occurred over the last day. I held the phone up to my ear.

"Hello."

I said, "Hi Dillon, I'm calling you back, what's up?" As I waited for his response, I pulled out my hands-free ear buds and popped them in.

"A couple of things, uh, how are you?"

I crossed my legs and sunk back into the couch. "Things are okay, I had a busy night."

"Are you okay? I saw something about a bust in a trafficking case on the news. Is it related to your case?"

I wondered if telling him was a good idea. I didn't exactly

like advertising my failures, but what the heck. He knew the story. "Yes, there was an arrest in the trafficking case. I've been in contact with the lead detective on the case and he called me to let me know about the bust before the news. I went down and watched as the suspect was taken into custody."

"Wow. That's major. How are you feeling about it?"

How was I feeling about it? Unsettled. The arrest was just step one. I wanted him to rot in jail for the rest of his life. "Mixed emotions. I'll be okay."

"That's good."

Filling the silence, "So, any news on KT? I saw the Facebook post."

"I also received an email and text, same sentiment."

At least it wasn't threatening his life or violent in nature. That was a relief. "Anything else?"

"No, not about KT."

About who? Oh, right. "About Taylor? Did you let her down easy?"

Hesitation by Dillon.

I didn't like that.

"Well, I haven't told her yet, but I will. I sort of made another study date with her for Wednesday, but I'll tell her before that. I think I'm going to be gentle and tell her it's for her own safety."

Uh, what? He made another date? Was this guy clueless with women or what? *Jeez.* "I don't think that's a good idea at all. Why did you make a date with her? That's the opposite of what you said you'd do. Unless...you don't want to stop seeing her?" Shoot. I hadn't considered that. He said he didn't but then again he made another date with her too. This guy was all over the place.

"No, that's not it. I don't want to hurt her feelings."

"Too late." That came out a bit harsher than I'd meant. But

come on! "Look, the more you lead her on, the worse it's going to be. If you think you might want to see her after this KT thing is resolved, then tell her it's for her safety. She should understand." Taylor didn't seem unreasonable. Her attitude changed quickly, but that was normal for a teenager, right?

"I don't want a relationship with her. I'll tell her tomorrow before we're supposed to meet."

Finally. *This guy.* "Good. Oh, and let me know when you do it, I want to call her and see if she's okay afterward. I have the feeling she isn't terribly experienced, and she seems sweet. She's actually helping with an investigation Martina is working on." *Right. I needed to call Taylor about that.*

"Okay."

"I'll talk to you later." I hung up before I heard him say good-bye. It had been too emotional of a day to have to deal with a clueless man, too. One last task on my list for the day and I could finally get some sleep. I looked up Taylor's number and hit send.

"Hello?"

"Hi Taylor, this is Selena."

"Oh, hi."

"I'm calling because the sketch artist confirmed the time for you to come in and give a description of Greg." We had texted a preliminary date and time, Taylor said she was open anytime and wanted to do everything she could to help find Kaitlyn. A pang of guilt hit me. She was about to be crushed by Dillon. Anyway, I looked at it, that sucked. I hope she took the news okay. Maybe I'd take her out after the sketch artist appointment and try to cheer her up, or at least be there to talk to. Who knows, maybe Taylor and I would become friends.

"Great. I'll see you in class."

"See you in class."

I hung up. Now, at last, my bed was screaming my name. I

propelled myself off the sofa, slogged over to my queen-size bed, and plopped face down. I could smell the lavender from the fabric softener and inhaled deeply. I shut my eyes and prayed I'd get some good sleep tonight and not have my dreams filled with blood and traffickers.

29

DILLON

I EXITED MY ABNORMAL PSYCH CLASS AND HEADED TOWARD the quad. My mind shifted to my conversation with Selena last night. I felt like I was really blowing it with her and I needed to fix it fast. She certainly wasn't a fan of my plan to tell Taylor I couldn't see her because of my stalker. Now, I had to create an alternative plan to tell her explicitly the two of us would not be involved romantically. I didn't want to risk any chance I may have with Selena one day.

Had she really been that mad that I was trying to blow off Taylor? I didn't quite get the big deal. My approach was pretty much standard practice with my guy friends, and I'd even been ghosted a time or two. Actually, yeah, it did kind of suck when it happened, but I knew what was going on and didn't dwell on it. I moved on. Why hadn't Taylor? If what Selena said was true and she wasn't very experienced with dating, that would explain it, I guess.

For Selena to get so annoyed, she must have never ghosted anyone before. I suppose I could see that. She was pretty upfront about what she will do and not do. Like, at first when she didn't want to help me find out who was stalking me. I liked that about her. There was no guesswork. If she wasn't happy about something, I had a feeling she would most certainly tell me - immediately, like she had with my plans to let Taylor down more gently.

She made me consider that that type of behavior may have caused this whole KT debacle. It was getting so freaky. If my past approach to ending romantic connections was the cause - lesson learned. I'd never do that again.

I continued up to the quad, wondering when the right time would be to talk to Taylor. I needed to figure out how I would tell her, so that she understood the message and could move on. I could do a complete honesty approach. I could tell her I was sorry, but I just wasn't interested in her in a girlfriend kind of way. Explain that it was because I thought she was too young. Was that the only reason? She was nice, and we had similar interests. She was really attractive. I guess it was that she was too young. She was still a teen, for Pete's sake. I couldn't even take her to a bar. Not that I was a big drinker, but if I wanted to go out to celebrate and have a few, she wouldn't be allowed in. Okay, it was settled, that was my story and I was sticking to it.

I pulled out my phone and texted Taylor.

Are you on campus?

Her response was almost immediate.

Yes

Are you free to talk?

Sure

Followed by a smiley face emoji.

Dang it. She thought the reason we were going to meet was something good. I didn't think it would be. My nerves rattled as I responded.

Meet in the library?

Perfect. I'm already here. See you soon.

Followed by another smiley face.

See you soon.

I zipped up my jacket and marched toward the library. It was about to get ugly. I reached the building and hurried up the steps. A student was exiting and held the door open for me, I thanked them and continued in.

I rubbed my hands together as I searched for Taylor. I

spotted her right away, sitting at a table by herself. My nerves rattled as I approached. "Hi."

A wide grin appeared. "Hi. Good to see you."

"You too." I took the seat across from her. I needed to be direct.

She gazed at me. "What is it you wanted to talk to me about?"

This was going to be harder than I thought. "I wanted to let you know I think you're great. You're nice, smart, and pretty, but I wanted to be very clear with you about my intentions, since it seems maybe you have the wrong idea about me. About us."

Her smile faded. "What do you mean?"

She was going to make me spit it out. "I'm not interested in you as a girlfriend. You're too young for me, but I hope that one day you'll find a great guy who will adore you - like you deserve. I'm sorry I should've been more upfront before. Can we still be friends?"

Taylor's mouth dropped open, and she shook her head, appearing flustered. She grabbed her books and laptop and shoved them in her bag. She didn't meet my gaze. "Sure, yeah, that's great. I forgot. I have to meet someone. Bye."

I watched as she ran off. I had a feeling she wasn't fine. I'd probably hurt her. I felt bad about that, but what's the point of continuing to see someone if you won't have a future with them? She'd be fine before too long. We only hung out the one time; I was sure she'd be over the whole thing in no time at all.

I let out the breath I'd been holding. Relief shot through me. It was done. I texted Selena.

Just talked to Taylor. All is loud and clear. It's done.

Selena responded.

Good.

Now that the Taylor situation was solved, all I needed to do was to get rid of KT and I'd be home free. Maybe then I'd finally have a shot at Selena. The woman I couldn't stop thinking about.

30

TAYLOR

I SETTLED DOWN ON THE BATHROOM FLOOR, TEARS streaming down my face as my chest heaved, trying to capture as much oxygen as possible. I shouldn't have sprinted back to my dorm, but I couldn't let him see what he had done to me. What she had done to me. I know this wasn't Dillon. We had chemistry and shared interests. It was her. That stupid bitch, Selena. She did this. She turned Dillon against me. C'mon, like Dillon really thought I was too young? No way. I was only a few years younger and I'm mature beyond my years. I shook my head back and forth as I realized the error of my ways. I'd known since the first time I had seen the two of them together that she would stand in the way of Dillon's and my future. And now she had.

I thought back to my date with Dillon, and how perfect together we were together. How the conversation flowed freely, and we discussed our favorite movies. Why didn't he realize we were meant to be together? It was so obvious.

I knew now that I needed to eliminate Selena from the picture. There was no other way. The only thing I didn't understand was why they kept talking to each other if they weren't dating. And why were they lying to me about it? It didn't make any sense at all. Why the lies, why the secrecy?

How could he possibly think she was more right for him? She was a tough investigator, not someone you brought home to your parents. I was that person. What had Selena said to him to turn him against me? Why did she hate me so much? I didn't understand it? Why was everyone against me?

Just like Kaitlyn. Well, not just like Kaitlyn, but she had turned on me too. We had been such good friends, but then her stupid boyfriend came along and I was toast. She'd insisted I was trying to ruin her happiness, but she was wrong. I was trying to look out for her. I could tell by the way he looked at her, and at me, that he was a lowlife. I am a good person; I wanted what was best for her. I want what is best for Dillon. I am what is best for him. I had to make him see.

I took a deep breath. I knew what I had to do. Selena was a poison and I would have to be the antidote.

I stood up and stepped toward the sink. I rinsed the razor blade and dried it off before setting it back into the case and into the drawer. I exited the bathroom and nearly jumped out of my skin.

"Hi Mandy. I didn't hear you come in."

She tipped her head toward me. "I heard you crying. Are you okay? Is it the guy? Did something happen?"

I nodded. "He told me he just wants to be friends." I felt proud of myself for not tearing up. He liked tough girls, well that was exactly what he was going to get - with me.

Mandy embraced me. "I'm so sorry," and then stepped back. "Did he give you a reason?"

I rolled my eyes. "Yes, he said I was too young. I didn't buy it though."

"No?"

"No. There is this girl in our class that I think has been talking bad about me."

"Really? That's terrible. You should confront her. That's not cool."

I had every intention of doing that very thing. I would get Dillon back. My phone buzzed. I glanced at the screen. Speaking of the devil. I looked back at Mandy. "I need to get this."

"No prob."

I walked toward my bed. "Hello."

"Hi Taylor, it's Selena. How are you?"

I chirped. "I'm great. How are you?"

I thought, *actually I'm terrible, but I'll be fine once I get rid of you.* She would not hear me cry or know that she had any effect on me. This was war and I was a warrior.

Selena hesitated. That bitch knew. She knew he dumped me. They were in cahoots. She finally said, "I'm doing well, thank you. I'm at the office with my stepmother, working on Kaitlyn's case, and I thought of you. I wanted to confirm the appointment time with the sketch artist was still okay?"

Yes, I was most certainly available, Selena. It was like magic. My entire plan unfolded in my mind. I knew exactly what I would do. "It's perfect."

"Great. Thank you so much, Taylor, we really appreciate your help."

"No, Selena. Thank you." I put the phone down on the coffee table. My heart skipped a beat and a smile spread across my face. I was one step closer to getting Dillon back.

31

SELENA

THE NEXT EVENING, I TAPPED MY FINGERS ON THE DESK AS I listened to Detective Brown through the speaker on my phone. He explained that the only charges that the district attorney was going to bring against Ocampo's boss, Honeywell, were human trafficking and kidnapping, but it wouldn't include Brendon's murder. It made little sense. Why couldn't they charge him? My blood felt like it was boiling. I couldn't just sit here and do nothing. "I understand they need evidence, but there must be fingerprints or something from the scene. There must be a trail from Honeywell to Ocampo. Have they checked phone records from the night of Brendon's death?"

"Everything they have on Brendon's death is circumstantial. We are fairly certain he was involved, but the DA is more concerned with putting him away for life. The theory is if we focus on the charges we know we can prove in court, like human trafficking and kidnapping, we will put this guy away. I know it's disappointing, but it's what we have to do to get this particular scumbag off the street."

Nobody cared about Brendon's murder but me? Is that what he was telling me? It made me sick to think that they would just

let this go. The murder of an upstanding citizen - a future extin-
guished. "Will they at least continue to investigate Brendon's
death so they might charge Honeywell later?"

"Right now, it's on the back burner. I'll let you know as the
case develops and Honeywell is brought to trial - if it goes to
trial. If it does, we may need you to testify about what you saw
with the two girls."

"I'll testify." I'd also bring up, on the stand, that he killed
Brendon if the district attorney failed to do so. "When will he be
arraigned?"

"He's on the docket for tomorrow. You're welcome to attend,
but I'm not sure it's in your best interest."

"Why not?"

"I was talking to your stepmother, Martina. She's okay with
you getting information on the case, but her and I both agree it's
not healthy to be obsessed with it either."

I can't believe Martina told him not to include me and
discussed what they thought was in my best interest. I was an
adult. I was twenty-one years old. I could drink alcohol or fight
in a war. I knew what was in my best interest. "Why don't you
go ahead and send over any related information and if my
schedule allows I'll attend."

There was silence on the other end before he finally said,
"I'll be in touch, Selena."

"Thanks." I hung up the phone and hoped he would relay
the information. I wanted Honeywell to see my face when he
was standing there, pathetic and alone. I didn't care if Martina
thought it was in my best interest or not, I was going. I appreciated her looking out for me, but she and I both knew there was a
point at which she had to let me make my own decisions. As if I
was summoning her in my thoughts, she appeared in my cubi-
cle. "Hi Martina."

"Hi. Did you get a call from the detective?"

"Yeah, I just got off the phone with him. Interestingly, he told me that he and you decided it was not in my best interest to be involved in the arraignment and that maybe I shouldn't be too close to the investigation or the trial unless they need me to testify."

Martina folded her arms. "I am only looking out for you, Selena. I don't think it's healthy for you to be so involved in this case. You have your entire life ahead of you. The police have him, you should let it go."

I interrupted her. "They're not even charging him for Brendon's murder. Sure, they'll put him in prison, but no one will be held accountable for what he did to Brendon."

"I think you need to proceed cautiously with this case. You have your entire life ahead of you. You'll be graduating soon and may be starting your own company. There are so many positive things to look forward to, it would do you well to stop looking backward." Martina glanced sideways. "Follow me into the conference room."

She didn't wait for a response, she simply marched toward the conference room. I didn't like how that felt. Not that I had a lot of choice in the matter, I headed towards the conference room wondering what dread was about to befall me. I couldn't always read Martina, but I knew we would not discuss something positive. I sensed a lecture coming on. I reached the room and shut the door behind me.

Martina stood next to the table on the far side of the room. I stepped closer but kept a suitable distance. She looked me dead in the eye. "I know you've been investigating the traffickers."

My heart raced. There it was. I hadn't covered my tracks as well as I thought. I suppose I'd been naïve to think I could keep that type of secret in an office full of private investigators. "If you knew, why haven't you said anything?"

Martina let out a breath and folded her arms. "Because most

of what you're doing is harmless. Tracking financial records and real estate dealings isn't anything illegal - although it is not within the spirit of our company policy. We don't investigate cases we're not assigned to. I think you know that. But what I don't think you realize is that anything you do reflects on me and my reputation at the company. If Stavros found out that you have been secretly investigating the traffickers, I don't know if I could protect you anymore. He owns 60% of the firm. I only own 40%. That's not the majority. He could vote you out and there wouldn't be anything I could do about it. To be honest, I said nothing because I figured if you were here and I knew what you were doing, I could keep an eye on you."

She'd known the entire time. Was I so blinded by my rage that I didn't see how foolish I had behaved? I shook my head. "Not that it even matters now. I didn't find him, the police did."

"Look, I talked to Detective Brown and they've been doing stake outs. I guess they've known about him for a while now, but they've been trying to collect evidence to catch him red-handed and ensure he goes away for a long time. The tactics the police employed: photographs, wiretaps, and stakeouts are all things you couldn't do, not on your own. And even if you tried, you wouldn't have done so by legal means, so even if you caught them, in all likelihood, they couldn't be prosecuted. You'll learn in this job that there're some things we simply can't do, and we need to leave it to the police. In some situations we absolutely can, but not in this case. You need to understand, we can't win them all. You have to learn to live with that."

I held my tongue. I knew she wasn't finished.

Martina unfolded her arms. "This job can be disappointing, but with the disappointment comes the triumphs too. We have reunited family members, we've taken people out of harm's way, and we've gathered evidence to help put bad guys away. That is what you have to focus on in this job or it will eat you up. You must know when to let it go - with grace. It's imperative in order to keep this job and your sanity." She stepped closer to me. "I hope you'll take this advice, Selena."

Did I have a choice? I nodded. "So you don't think I should be involved in the trial?"

"Attend if you must, but there is the possibility he might plead out. For everyone's sake, I hope he does. Trials can be a nightmare. Hopefully, he'll take a plea and you can start your career with a clean slate. A fresh start. You'll do great, Selena, but you also need to know your limitations. We all have them."

Martina didn't seem to have any. "I just don't know if that's true. I mean, look at you. What limitations do you have?"

She shook her head, and her body relaxed. "Selena, I have limitations. You forget, I'm an addict. Every day I struggle to keep sober. I almost lost my life and ruined others because of my addiction. And I see that as a limitation, but at the same time our limitations can also be a strength. I see that now. Through my addiction, I saw I could reach rock bottom. At the bottom, I learned to be grateful for all my blessings and to accept what I can't change or control. It's been over a decade since I've had a drink, but there isn't a day I don't think about picking up a bottle. Especially on the hard days. We all struggle."

I had never asked Martina about her addiction. I knew she was an addict like my dad, but I didn't know what her poison was. I guess it's easy to turn someone into a hero when you don't know their flaws. But we all have flaws, Martina was right about that. We all have our inner demons that we fight each day. For Martina it's alcohol and for me it's my inability to let go. I bit my lower lip, contemplating my future. Could I move on with grace, or would I always fall down, crippled by my own demons? "Thank you for sharing that with me, Martina. I value your opinion. I think sometimes I forget you have your own demons."

Martina nodded.

"How are things going with Kaitlyn's case?"

"Well, as you know we have the sketch artist scheduled with Taylor to get a picture of Greg and hopefully an ID. Right now, it's our only lead."

"I hope Kaitlyn's okay."

"Me too."

I was about to leave when my phone buzzed. I picked it up. I mouthed to her, "It's Taylor."

"Hello, Selena Bailey here."

"This is Taylor, how are you?"

"I'm fine. What's up?"

"Well, when we spoke yesterday, I completely spaced. I don't have a car, is there anyway you could pick me up? I know it's a huge favor to ask."

"Sure, I'll head out now, just text me your address."

"I'm in the Towers."

"I didn't realize that. I lived there my first year too."

"What a coincidence. Well, thank you. I appreciate it."

I hung up and said to Martina, "I need to go pick up Taylor. She doesn't have a car."

Martina gave a quizzical look. "Okay, see you later."

I exited the conference room, feeling better now that Martina and I didn't have any secrets between us.

32

SELENA

I TURNED UP THE RADIO TO LISTEN TO SOME TUNES ON THE way to pick up Taylor. I bobbed my head to the beat of the song. It wasn't exactly my favorite song but Katy Perry's *Part of Me* was pretty catchy. My phone buzzed, and I threw a quick glance over to the passenger seat. Dillon calling again.

I hadn't talked to him since he had texted me that he'd told Taylor he just wanted to be friends. My mind had been elsewhere with the trafficking case.

After Taylor and I met with the sketch artist and had dinner, I planned to review the footage from the library, assuming there weren't any new posts from KT.

I hadn't checked yet today. She hadn't as of yesterday, which was why I had put off reviewing the video footage. KT's daily posts and texts and messages to Dillon had stopped over the last 24 hours. It was strange, actually. Maybe KT had gotten bored and moved on. Either way, I should follow up with Dillon.

What the heck. I turned off the song and accepted the call while placing him on speaker. "Hi, this is Selena Bailey." I answered using my full name to prepare for having my own private investigations firm and would receive calls from potential clients. Paying clients. The idea was super exciting. So many things going on that were exciting and sad and troubling. Too many emotions.

"Hi, Selena."

"What's going on? I hear a lot of commotion in the background."

"The police are at my apartment, I received another gift from KT."

Uh, oh. "What kind of gift?"

"I'm afraid this one wasn't as sweet as the candy. There's blood all over my bedroom."

A blood-soaked bedroom was a far cry from a box of chocolates. "What do you mean there is blood all over your bedroom? Is somebody hurt? Are you hurt?"

Thoughts were racing through my mind. Had I dropped the ball and failed to keep Dillon safe? Clearly something had triggered KT. Did she see us meeting at school a few days ago? It was so early in the morning; I had doubted anyone would get up that early.

"No, it's just blood. I don't see any animals or any people - just blood splashed all over my bed and on the walls."

"Any idea if it's human blood or not?"

"Cops say they won't know until it gets tested in the lab, which they said they'd do right away. I think they're finally taking this situation seriously."

Small favors. "I was going to run an errand, but I'll stop by your place first. I should be there pretty soon."

"Okay, thanks Selena. It's appreciated."

I didn't like the shakiness in his voice. He was scared, and I felt responsible. "Are you okay?" Why had I thought KT had found more interesting things to do than to harass Dillon? Or allow myself to think she'd move on after threatening his life? *Way to drop the ball, Selena.*

"I'll be okay. I guess."

"We can talk when I get there. I'm sorry this happened. See you soon."

It may be time to suggest Dillon see a professional counselor. The amount of trauma he was enduring must be taking its toll. I'd stay with him until we came up with a plan. Maybe he could stay with his parents. Or with me - or a friend. He shouldn't be alone, not after something so horrifying.

Shoot, I needed to tell Taylor that I couldn't pick her up. Maybe somebody from the office could. As soon as I pulled into Dillon's driveway. I texted Taylor.

So sorry. I'm caught up in an emergency. Call the offices of Drakos Monroe. Someone will be able to pick you up.

I felt terrible not being there, but it sounded like this thing at Dillon's was bad and right now, it appeared he needed me more than Taylor did.

33

SELENA

I walked up the path to Dillon's apartment as some police officers were leaving. Officer Heller was one of them. He stopped me. "Hi Selena. Glad you're here. He needs you. It's a mess in there and he's pretty shaken up."

"Thanks." I suppressed a snipe about how if he'd taken the case seriously maybe we wouldn't be in this situation right now.

"Be careful, this type of escalation rarely ends well."

Thanks for the tip. "Okay. Talk to you later." And I continued past until I reached Dillon's front door. I knocked lightly. I didn't want to startle him since he'd already had a bit of a day - to put it mildly.

The door creaked open until I met his gaze. It looked like he was about to cry. Poor guy. "May I come in?"

He silently stepped back and fully opened the door. I entered and gave him what I thought was a much needed hug. He apprehensively wrapped his strong arms around me. He was shaking ever so slightly. I didn't pull away until I thought he was ready.

He said sheepishly, "Thanks."

I looked at the front door handle. They had dusted for

prints again. What a mess. I continued on into the living room and to the kitchen, which was seemingly undisturbed, before turning left down the hallway where he led me to the doorway of his bedroom. I didn't step in - it wasn't necessary. I could see from the doorway that it was like a scene out of a horror movie. There was a lot of blood. The bed was drenched, and the walls were splattered as if it was an eccentric modern art exhibit. "When did you come home to find this?"

"I got home thirty minutes ago, and it was like this."

"Where's your roommate?"

"He's at his parents' house. It's his dad's 50th birthday or something. He went home yesterday."

"Did you install the cameras?"

"Sort of. I gave the police a copy of the video I had."

"What do you mean, sort of? Was the person who did this on the video?"

He shook his head. "No, I didn't install cameras in my bedroom, only in the hallways, the entry, and in the common spaces. The police think that they, the person who did this, came into my bedroom through the window."

I told him cameras in every room, but I suppose he didn't want to invade his own privacy. I guess I could understand that. It would be strange to be on camera while you slept. "What about the alarms? You had one on the window, right? Did the cops ask the neighbors if they heard the alarm?"

"The police said they would ask the neighbors if they heard or saw anything, but when I came home, the alarm wasn't on."

I carefully stepped into the bedroom, tiptoeing around the blood on the carpet and over to the window. The gray dust from the fingerprinting process was everywhere. The alarm was intact. Which indicates that KT likely slid the window open, heard the alarm, climbed in, and shut the window right away.

When finished with her 'work', an equally fast exit would have concealed anything out of the ordinary.

It wasn't like the alarms were exactly high tech. If the window opened it went off, if it were closed it was shut off. It wasn't connected to a phone system. It was simply to alert the inhabitants that someone was trying to get in. If the person was quick, they would have had only a few seconds of the alarm sounding. The alarm itself wasn't particularly loud, but a prolonged amount of time would alert somebody inside, but since nobody was home, there was nobody to alert.

I swiveled around to survey the carnage. There was nothing scribbled on the walls, no message, just blood. Strange. A warning, maybe? The splatter was haphazard and the large pool of blood on the bed looked like it was dumped from a bucket. My estimation was the entire scene could've been created in less than a minute. A single minute to craft a scene of pure rage. We were dealing with a disturbed individual, no doubt. I looked over at Dillon. "Any messages from KT?"

"I got a text."

"What does it say?"

"My heart beats for you."

Poetic. Creepy, but poetic. A knock on the door startled both of us. We exchanged glances. "Are you expecting anyone?"

"No. Maybe it's the police, they said they'd question the neighbors."

"Did they say they'd return today?"

"No."

I looked at the blood and then back at Dillon. I didn't like the feel of this. "I'll answer the door."

He protested. "I can get the door. I can handle myself."

"Look, I have self-defense training and know how to spot danger. I've got this. Trust me." I hurried past him and toward the front door. I looked through the peephole and then stepped back. What? That made little sense. Why was she here? How did she get here? She said she didn't have a car. "Were you expecting Taylor?"

"Taylor? No."

Strange. I looked at him, put a finger up to my mouth, motioning for him to be quiet. I opened the door halfway. "Hi. Taylor. What a surprise. What are you doing here?"

"Oh, I talked to your office, and they said I could find you here. I hope that's okay, I had my neighbor drop me off. I was kind of scared to go to the sketch artist by myself. I hope it's okay that I came here, I figured after you were done doing whatever you were doing you could come with me to the sketch artist."

Something wasn't right about this. I hadn't told anybody at the office I was heading to Dillon's. I should have, but I didn't. "Who from my office said that I was here?"

Taylor looked past me toward Dillon. "Can I come in? It's freezing out here." She gritted her teeth, chattering them as if she were literally freezing. I looked her up and down.

Dillon stepped forward. "Sure, come in."

Taylor stepped in and I had to lean against the wall to not get trampled. It was as if I were invisible. She didn't seem threatening. Not physically, but something was off, I could feel it in my bones.

She shut the door behind her and then lifted her hand up to her face. "What's that all over your door handle?" She asked as she marched toward Dillon, who was leaning against the kitchen counter.

I followed behind and explained. "It's fingerprint dust."

Ignoring my presence, she eyed Dillon. "Really? Did somebody break into your apartment?"

Dillon said, "Yeah, earlier."

She placed her hand on his shoulder. "You poor thing. Did they take anything?"

"No."

I looked at Dillon and Taylor. Dillon seemed to tense at her touch. There was definitely some tension between them, but Taylor was acting as if they were besties. He said he'd had the talk with her. Maybe she had been fine about them being just friends. She told me she was great when I asked her how she was. Yet, my gut told me something was very wrong here. *Holy moly. It couldn't be. Could it?*

"Hey Taylor, Dillon and I are about done here. Why don't you and I head to the office?"

I gave Dillon a knowing look. He cocked his head as if confused by my nonverbal clues.

Taylor let go of Dillon and turned toward the kitchen, peering over the breakfast bar. "That smells amazing. Is the coffee fresh? I'd kill for a cup of coffee."

Yikes.

"Um, yeah. Let me get you a cup." Dillon walked around to the interior of the kitchen and grabbed a mug. "Selena, do you want one?"

"No, I'm fine, thanks."

I watched Taylor follow Dillon into the kitchen. She was now so close to him she was practically on top of Dillon as he carefully picked up the carafe and poured the coffee into the cup. He handed it to her, and she took a sip, placing it down onto the countertop. "Yummy. Thank you. That's so sweet of you."

I stepped closer to the entrance of the kitchen. She was acting very odd. A mix of calm and deranged. "Taylor, maybe we should go, the sketch artist is expecting you."

Taylor blinked her eyes and smiled. "I think we'll have to reschedule. It's so cozy here. I don't want to leave."

"Uh, it's actually not a good time. I have a lot of cleanup to do."

She turned to Dillon. "Oh?"

"Yeah, someone broke in and poured blood everywhere. You don't want to see it, it's quite disturbing."

Taylor flung her hands to her chest. "My gosh! That's horrible. I'll stay and help cleanup."

Interesting.

Dillon stammered. "Uh."

Useless.

"Taylor, let's leave Dillon alone. I don't think he wants company right now."

She glared at me. "And you know what Dillon wants? I'm sure you do."

Uh-oh.

"Taylor, I think you should leave. Or should I call you KT?"

Dillon's eyes popped wide open.

Taylor reached her hand into her coat pocket and pulled out a revolver. She aimed it at me. "I'm not going anywhere and neither are you."

34

SELENA

I INSTINCTIVELY PUT MY HANDS UP IN THE AIR. "TAYLOR, what are you doing? Why are you doing this?"

KT revealed.

The pieces slowly fell into place in my mind. The Facebook posts stopped after Dillon told her he wanted to be just friends. Yet, Taylor still saw me as a romantic rival or her enemy for whatever reason she had concocted. She'd been following both of us. She vandalized my car. She threatened Dillon's life. I needed to try to reason with her or this situation would end badly for Dillon and me.

Taylor waved the gun at the two of us. "Both of you sit over there - at the dining table."

I eyed Dillon, encouraging him to follow her orders. You didn't question somebody with a gun in her hands - not unless you had a death wish. Dillon sat on one end of the table and I on the other. I didn't dare sit next to Dillon and appear as if we were together because it might set her off.

She swaggered over toward the table. "Let's talk about the situation, shall we?"

Dillon shook his head in disbelief. "Taylor, why are you

doing this? I don't understand this at all. Is this because you're mad at me?"

Did he really not understand Taylor was KT?

Taylor shook her head. "No, sweetheart. Of course not. I'm trying to show you what I already know. I know you felt it too. From the very first day we met, I knew we were about to embark on a special journey together. That was until she..." Taylor glared at me before refocusing on Dillon. "Came along and distracted you. She poisoned your mind and turned you against me. She isn't the right girl for you. I am. She's in our way. She's the villain in our love story, but don't worry sweetheart, I am willing to be the hero and defeat her to ensure our future happiness."

I didn't like the sound of that. It sounded like Taylor thought killing me would get her closer to Dillon. Martina and Dee were right. She had to have serious mental health issues. How had I not seen it before? I needed to find a method of reasoning with her, even it was completely false. *Ah, ha.* I said, voice shaking, "Taylor, it isn't true. Dillon doesn't love me. He loves you, he told me. The only reason he stopped seeing you was because he needed to study more so that he could secure your future. His love for you is so strong it was distracting him. Isn't that right Dillon?" I looked to Taylor and then Dillon.

Dillon sat there like a deer caught in the headlights. Maybe he was in shock. It was likely the first time someone threatened him with a gun - not everyone reacted well to that type of situation. He choked out a "Yes, Taylor, it's true. I think you're great. I just need to get through my LSAT preparation and then we can go out again. You're right, I felt it that first day too."

"You did?" Taylor asked.

I wasn't sure she was buying it. I said, "See Taylor, there's no reason for any of this. Dillon is yours. I've been helping him with a project, that's all."

Her face soured. "Oh, really? What exactly were you working on? Dillon is a straight 'A' student and doesn't need your help. When will the lies end Selena?"

"I'm not lying." She knew Taylor was KT, so no reason to hold back the truth now. I shook my head and tried to relax. "You want the truth, Taylor? I'll give you the truth. Dillon knew I had been an investigator, and he needed me to help him figure out who was leaving him messages, gifts, and breaking into his apartment. I've been trying to figure out KT's identity, so they could meet. But maybe I should've asked for your help. You know who KT is, don't you, Taylor?"

She paced and shook her head, ignoring my inference. "Well, if that's true, then why did I see you at the café, laughing and having a grand old time? Why won't Dillon go out with me again? I don't buy your story. Why would he say I'm too young?" She stop pacing and focused on me with fury in her eyes. "Truth? I don't believe a word that comes out of your stupid mouth."

Was she was having some sort of break? I needed to do something and fast. "Dillon, I've told her the truth, please explain to her what you told me." This guy better have understood the hint I was practically screaming in his face. He needed to pretend to be in love with her, or neither one of us would get our happily ever after.

35

DILLON

I was right, this girl was completely nuts. Now I have to pretend to love her so she doesn't kill Selena, or me, or both of us. And where the heck did she get a gun? How did she know Selena would be at my place? Had she followed Selena? Or had she never left after what she did to my bedroom? This entire scene was blowing my mind. How had this happened? Was it because I never called Taylor after the first time we'd met? Had Selena been right all along - and me 'ghosting' her caused all of this?

I mustered all of my courage and pleaded with Taylor. "It's true, Taylor. KT was following me, sending me messages. Some were threatening. I didn't know who it was or if KT was dangerous. You're right, the day we met, you captivated me with your smile and the sparkle in your eyes. The way you're strong and soft at the same time. I could tell you have an inner strength that I'm so attracted to. But once I started getting these strange and threatening messages, I thought maybe you'd be in danger if I started dating you. That's why I had to tell you we couldn't date. It was for your protection. I don't think I could forgive myself if something bad happened to you." I eyed Selena to assess my act.

She nodded slightly.

I continued. "That's the reason I pushed you away. I'm so sorry. I didn't want to push you away. At lunch, I felt it. I know you felt it too. You want to be an actress. I want to be an entertainment lawyer. Could there be a better match? No way. You and I together would be a dream team. If I understand correctly, you are the one behind the messages? I have to admit, it was so flattering. If I'm right, there is no longer a reason for us to be apart. Is that right? You're KT?"

Taylor stared at him, as if assessing whether he was a threat. "You really mean it?"

"Are you KT?"

She nodded with a tear rolling down her cheek. "It was me. It was always me."

"What does KT mean?"

She smiled like a gremlin that had been fed after midnight. "Kisses Taylor."

This was so whacked out, but it seemed to work. "That's sweet. Then there's no threat, you and I can date. We can be together."

I heard the skid of the chair across the linoleum. Taylor did too. We both looked over at Selena, who appeared to be getting ready to leap out of her chair. Taylor slowly studied my face and then back up at Selena. She raised the gun and pointed at Selena. "What are you trying to pull? You're lying to me. Aren't you?" She swung her body around and now had the gun directed at my face. "Are you lying to me?"

"No, Taylor, I'm not lying. I know this sounds corny, but I feel like with you — it was love at first sight."

Her arm wielding the gun relaxed. "You do?" Taylor grinned and then looked over at Selena and back at me again. Her eyes were wild "What about her? It seems like she's in the way, don't you think?"

"No, not at all. She was helping me find you. The KT part of you. Now that she has, she can go. Taylor, we'll have her leave and then you and I can finally spend some proper time together. Alone."

"You mean it?"

I nodded. I reached out my hand for Taylor to give me hers. I gazed into her eyes. "I love you, Taylor."

From the corner of my eye, I saw Selena about to push off from her chair. I hoped she was preparing to attack Taylor and get that gun away from her before she killed us all.

36

SELENA

I BRACED MYSELF, CLUTCHING ONTO THE EDGE OF THE dining table as I watched Taylor's reaction to Dillon. Dillon spoke quickly while wearing beads of sweat on his temples. I didn't envy either of the two actors in the scene. It was ironic they both wanted their respective futures in the world of drama and theater. Taylor clearly believed her delusions so much so that if she weren't currently holding us hostage, I'd believe her to be the damsel in distress. Dillon on the other side, playing the role of his life, that of a man in love and not a man pleading for his life. It was sad and terrifying at the same time.

A pain shot through the front of my head at the memory of playing a role similar to the one Dillon was now forced to play. The pain faded as I recalled my own trauma. When I had been held hostage, the first time, by my boyfriend Zeek, it took me a few hours before I realized my life was actually in danger. It hadn't occurred to me until we'd arrived at a remote cabin in Lake Tahoe. A place where nobody would hear me scream. The only reason I survived was that I'd pretended to go along with his sick homemaker fantasy, and when I began kissing him, I tried to attack him, hoping for the element of surprise. He was surprised but had still managed to get the upper hand. If the police - and Martina - hadn't arrived when they did, I'd be a goner.

Unfortunately, unless Dillon could do a better job than I had with Zeek, I didn't think there was a peaceful way out of this. It was becoming increasingly clear to me that the only way I would be able to diffuse the situation was by using good old-fashioned brute force. I just needed her distracted enough by Dillon to jump into action.

As I watched Dillon plead with her, I wondered how I'd missed Taylor's violent tendencies. I'd never gotten a dangerous vibe from her. Although I had watched her change moods rather quickly, which I found a bit jarring. But weren't mood swings normal in teens? I'd assumed she was simply a young, naïve freshman away for the first time. Boy, had I been wrong. Now she was a gun-wielding hostage taker hopelessly in love with Dillon, a man who barely knew her.

The mystery of KT's identity was finally solved. Yet the case was far from over. Could this all have been avoided if after that volunteer fair he had said that he wasn't interested? Maybe? Or maybe it wouldn't have made a difference. What else could I have done to have prevented this? Where had I gone wrong?

I studied Dillon. I tried to use my eyes to tell him to keep going. I don't know if it worked. I needed Taylor to keep her full attention on Dillon. She appeared suspicious but captivated by his words. This was my chance. A chance to save myself and Dillon. Maybe even save Taylor. If the cops arrived, they'd likely shoot to kill her in order to save us.

It had been a long time since I'd done any combat fighting in a live situation. I evaluated my target. She was taller than me but probably didn't have my skills. *Damn.* Why hadn't I tucked my baton in my coat or pocket? I had gotten lax and kept it in my backpack. *Never again.*

I watched the gun, which she held casually on me while her eyes were on Dillon. I didn't like it. She was distracted, but not enough. I was going to have to be fast.

Three...two...one.

I pushed the chair back and ducked under the table. I reached for her legs to bring her down. Taylor fell back, but caught herself on the breakfast bar behind her. She repositioned the gun until it was aimed inches from my face. "Don't fucking move."

Damn. My element of surprise had failed. My body froze in place, my heart thumping in my chest.

She shouted. "Get up."

I scrambled to my feet.

"Get back in the chair."

I walked backward toward the chair and slowly sat down, praying she didn't shoot me right then and there. A person with an unstable mind is not one that you wanted to have pointing a gun at you.

She waved the gun at me and then stepped closer. She pressed the muzzle of the gun to my temple. The cold metal sent shivers down my spine. She was really going to do it.

Of all the dangerous situations I'd found myself in, it would be a deranged love-sick 18-year-old from Walnut Creek that ended me. Not my mother's murderous boyfriend or my murderous boyfriend or a sexual sadist or human traffickers. It would be this blonde bombshell in love with a classmate. What was that saying? Right. No good deed went unpunished. If there was a God, she certainly had an ironic sense of humor.

I squeezed my eyes shut, trying to figure out my next move, assuming I had any time left. "Taylor, I know you love Dillon and I can appreciate that. I'm happy for the two of you if you want to be together, I will not stand in your way. But please don't end my life because not only will it end my life, but yours as well. The police will know it was you. Do you really think Dillon will love a killer? I have my whole life ahead of me, which I plan to dedicate to helping other people. Do you really want to take that away? Do you?" She didn't move the gun away from my head. "Well, do you?"

She now aimed the gun at Dillon. "Do you really love me, Dillon? Would you love me if I were a killer? Is it flattering that I would kill for you? Do you understand that is how much I love you? I love you so much that I would kill the kind of person who just wants to help other people? I would do it for us. But I have to know, if it's worth it to you. I will ask you one more time. Dillon, do you love me?"

Taylor was now sobbing, probably hoping that this man, whom I was fairly certain she barely knew, loved and accepted her. It was sad, and part of me felt sorry for her, but neither of those changed the fact that I was going to have to take her down.

37

TAYLOR

TEARS STREAMED DOWN MY CHEEKS AS I STARED AT Dillon. He wasn't answering me. Did he love me? Did he?

My heart was heavy. I knew the answer. I'd known the answer.

He didn't.

Through my tears, I looked down at the gun in my hand. What was I doing? I glanced at Dillon and then Selena - both wore terrified expressions.

Why wouldn't they? They'd been held hostage and had a gun shoved in their faces.

Why had I done this? "This is all wrong, so wrong." I muttered. "Dillon doesn't love me. Of course not. I'm so sorry." I shook my head and refocused on Selena. Her terror had switched to confusion. "Selena, I'm so sorry. For this. For everything. I'm so sorry. Please forgive me." I began sobbing uncontrollably. Heaving, I looked at both of them. Neither moved from their seat. Of course not. They were afraid of me. I had a gun. I had done terrible things. *Terrible*. Why? Why did I do this? Why couldn't I control it? What was wrong with me?

I tried to live without pharmaceuticals, despite my therapist's warnings. I hadn't taken my medication in months. This was all my fault.

All of it.

All of it was my fault.

I didn't want to live like this anymore. I couldn't. Maybe I needed to save other people and not think of myself. Like Selena. I was dangerous to them. I didn't want to hurt them. I didn't want to hurt anybody. "I'm so sorry, I don't want to hurt anybody." I wouldn't. I wouldn't let myself. Not anymore.

I shut my eyes before slowly lifting the gun and pressing the barrel to my chest.

38

SELENA

"Oh my God, no!" I kicked my chair back and reached overhead, punching at Taylor's arm before tackling her to the ground. I screamed at Dillon. "Take the gun."

I straddled Taylor, pinning her arms to the ground as she sobbed. She didn't fight me. She didn't try to move. This was a young woman in dire need of a mental health professional. She was in crisis. How had nobody seen it? I looked up at Dillon, who held the gun apprehensively in his fingers as if touching it would make it go off and kill all of us. "Set the gun down on the breakfast bar at the far end, away from us."

He nodded and hurried toward the end of the bar.

"Good. Now call the police."

I looked back down at Taylor, who continued to cry and mumble. "I'm so sorry" over and over again.

A pang of guilt shot through me. I'd been so angry that she vandalized my car, threatened Dillon, and used Brendon to get to me, I wanted to destroy her. To take her out permanently. I hadn't stopped to think that maybe all of her actions were a cry for help.

I hadn't thought about what had driven KT to a point in

their life that they were threatening strangers. I didn't want to hurt Taylor, but I could tell she wanted to hurt herself. I glanced up again at Dillon, who had his phone pressed to his ear, explaining the situation to the police. I looked down at Taylor. "Taylor, everything is going to be okay."

She rocked her head back and forth. "No, it's not. Why couldn't you just let me die? I don't want to hurt anyone ever again. I'm so sorry."

"You have a lot to live for. You don't have to hurt people. There are people who can help you."

She stopped moving and looked up at me. "They tried to help me. They tried. It didn't take. I still have these thoughts and can't control them. When I stood there and realized I had a gun in my hand, I couldn't believe it. It was like somebody else had come in here and took you hostage with a gun."

I contemplated whether I should ease up on my hold of her, but it was probably better safe than sorry. Hopefully, the police would get here soon so they could take her somewhere she could get help, like a mental hospital. I didn't think she'd do well in a jail cell. "Who tried to help you, Taylor?"

"My therapist. She gave me pills. When I started college, I stopped going to my therapist and stopped taking the pills. I didn't like the way they made me feel. They made me feel like I was a crazy person." Tears continued streaming down the sides of her face, dripping to the floor, but her breathing had steadied.

"Taylor, taking medication doesn't make you a crazy person. If you had cancer, you'd take chemotherapy drugs, right? It's the same thing. You have an illness that requires medication, just like cancer. You're not crazy." The irony was Taylor was the one who wanted to be an actress, yet here Dillon and I were putting on the performance of our lives. But then again, she'd been so good at covering her tracks, fooling all of us into thinking she was a normal young woman. Had she stalked before? Had she done something to her friend Kaitlyn?

Taylor sniffled. "Do you really think that?"

I nodded. "You're going to be okay, but I'm going to keep you like this until the police arrive, okay?"

She whispered, "Okay."

I watched this poor, sick young woman. Beautiful, bright, and engaged in the fight of her life. It was one thing to wage war on another person, but to battle your own mind was rough.

Taylor stared at the ceiling as I watched her expression. Anguish. Pain. It was heartbreaking. I didn't know what else to say to her, she'd nearly killed me and Dillon. And herself. The feelings I was having were complex; I'd never once felt sorry for any of my enemies in the past. It was strange, but there was just something about her sadness that I couldn't shake.

Dillon approached. "They should be here soon. Are you okay?" I looked down at Taylor, who shut her eyes and turned her head to the side. I glanced up at him. "I'm fine. Taylor is fine. We'll all be fine." A white lie? His face was still a few shades lighter than it was before Taylor had arrived. "Are you okay?"

"Yeah, I'm just a little..."

"Understandable."

He kneeled down, but Taylor refused to look at him.

"Taylor, I'm sorry if I caused this. I'm sorry I made you feel so bad. I should've been honest with you from the beginning."

I looked him in the eyes and shook my head back and forth. It wasn't the time, and it wasn't why she had done this. I was no psychiatrist, but Taylor had issues well before she ever had met Dillon.

My attention shifted toward the entrance of the apartment. Boots on the pavement. Radio static and clanking metal, followed by a loud bang on the door. The calvary had arrived. "Police, open up."

Dillon rushed over to the door and opened it. They came in, guns drawn. Dillon's eyes were wide, but he'd had the where-with-all to point at the gun on the breakfast bar and keep his hands up.

They rushed toward me, grabbing me in a swift motion before putting me in handcuffs. The other officer brought Taylor to her feet and cuffed her as well. I didn't resist.

The officer shouted over at Dillon. "Who had the gun?"

Taylor with head tilted down, a curtain of blonde hair covering half of her face. She softly said, "It was me. Please let Selena go."

I looked up at the officer and shrugged. It was protocol; it was fine. They got a distress call that a woman with a gun was holding two people hostage. They didn't know who was who.

They were going to need lengthy statements from all of us. It was going to be a long night.

The officer turned toward Taylor.

Freed from the cuffs, I interjected as they were about to start questioning her. "Officer, my name is Selena Bailey, and this is Taylor March. While I had her, Taylor explained to me she's typically under the care of a physician and on medication for a mental health issue. She's currently not on her meds."

The officer standing in front of Taylor met Taylor's gaze. "Ma'am, is that correct?"

She nodded without a word.

"Ma'am, I need you to say it aloud. Is that correct? Are you on any type of medication?"

She stared at the world's least friendly officer. "Yes, I used to be on meds and see a therapist. I'm not currently on anything."

Some bedside manner, dude. But to be fair, he was talking to somebody who came in with a gun and held two people hostage. Still, Taylor clearly wasn't a threat to anyone right now. He could ease up a bit. He stood with a wide stance, hands on hips. "Ma'am can you tell me what happened here?"

Taylor stared at the ground.

"Ma'am, we'll get you some help. It'll be okay, but we need to hear what happened first."

At least he wasn't a total jerk.

"Can I sit down?" She said with the tiniest of voices.

I eyed the two burly officers, giving them my best judgey look.

They removed the cuffs, gently sat her down on the chair, then cuffed her hands in front of her.

With a look of defeat in her eyes, Taylor began. "Thank you. I'll tell you everything you want to know."

"Let's start from the beginning. Let's talk about your illness and then what happened here tonight, okay?"

"You might want to take a seat." She gave a weak smile before lowering her gaze. "I've been under the care of a physician since high school. The therapist says that I suffer from major depressive disorder and borderline personality disorder. I was taking medication, but I stopped a few months ago, nobody knew that I stopped. I've never done anything like this before. I remember buying the gun and thinking that if I got Selena out of the way, Dillon would forget about her and fall in love with me instead. I didn't want to kill her. I came over here thinking I would scare them bad enough to vow they'd never see one another again." She shook her head. "It's sounds so stupid and crazy now." She let out a breath. "I was supposed to meet Selena earlier. I was supposed to go to her office to meet with a sketch artist. I called her and told her I didn't have a car and needed a ride. My plan was to threaten her on the drive over, but when she canceled, I decided to head over to Dillon's to see if she was there. If not, I'd comfort Dillon when he explained that someone broke in. I thought he'd see how much I cared, and that he'd see I was good for him. Stupid, I know. I came in, showed them my gun and then made them sit at the table. I didn't think it through. Obviously." She recounted the entire event. She didn't leave out any details except one.

The officer questioning Taylor looked at us. "Is that about right?"

"She missed the last part. She then turned the gun on herself, and that's when I tackled her. Officer, she is a risk to herself. She needs help."

The officer turned around and gave a nod to the officer behind him.

The small apartment was now filled with a dozen officers milling about. We stood there as they continued to question Taylor taking her information and then question us a few minutes later. I glanced over at the entry to the apartment and my body relaxed. Lieutenant Tippin strutted over to Dillon and me. "Selena, are you all right?"

"I'm fine."

"Thank goodness. I called Martina when I heard you were involved in the hostage situation. I let her know, and she told me she's on her way."

"Thank you."

Dillon cocked his head at me.

"Martina, my stepmother, knows all the police around here." I explained.

Tippin studied Dillon. "This is the friend you were helping? The one with the stalker?"

"Yes. We believe Taylor was the stalker."

Taylor turned around. "I'm so sorry."

I gave her a pitiful smile. I hadn't realized she was listening to us. I waved Tippin over to the other side of the apartment. Dillon followed behind. "She turned the gun on herself. She was going to kill herself until I tackled her and got the gun away.

I don't know the protocol, but she can't go to regular jail. She told us she's been diagnosed with depression and a personality disorder. She's off her medication. She needs to be in a medical facility. If she ends up in county, she may not survive."

He scratched his chin and then nodded. "Don't worry. We'll take care of her. Are you sure you're okay?"

"A little rattled, but I'll be fine. I've been through worse."

"Really?"

"Long story short, danger seems to follow me wherever I go."

"Have you considered trying to stay away from danger?"

I grinned. "No."

Tippin chuckled. "That's what I thought."

We were interrupted by the rapid succession of feet running towards us. I looked past Tippin. My eyes locked with Martina's. She continued until she reached me. Without a word, she wrapped her arms around me and squeezed tighter than I'd ever been squeezed. She gently pushed me back. "Are you okay?"

"Yes, I'm fine." And I would be. This was a good lesson. Never let my guard down or be unarmed. My baton fit in my back pocket, so why did I stop putting it there? It had been completely useless hidden away in my backpack.

I recounted the entire story to Martina. Maybe it would be more efficient to record it and play it for anyone who asked? It was exhausting to retell every excruciating detail. Martina turned to Dillon. "You must be Dillon?"

"Yes."

I shook my head. "Sorry, I didn't even think to introduce you. Martina, this is Dillon, the classmate I was helping."

Dillon extended a hand. "Nice to meet you. I mean, under the circumstances."

Martina ignored his hand and embraced him in a hug. She

stood back a few moments later. "I'm glad you're okay. Do you have family nearby?"

"Yeah, they're not far."

"Are you close?"

"Yes."

"You should call them. You'll probably want to go home for a while. This is a traumatic experience, you'll want to have the security of family. I'll also forward Selena the names of a few good therapists who help survivors of trauma."

"Oh, I don't..." He attempted to protest.

Rookie. There was no resisting Martina.

She continued. "Trust me. Call your parents and make an appointment with a therapist. What you've been through is traumatic and can have lasting effects like PTSD or sleep issues." Martina eyed me. "Be sure he calls someone."

"Will do." He may not realize how traumatic the experience really was, but I fully agreed with Martina, he was going to need to talk to someone. I glanced over at the dining table where they continued to question Taylor, but from the looks of it, they'd shifted to a more gentle approach. One officer handed her a tissue, and she thanked him as tears streamed down her cheeks. There would need to be a lot of healing for those in this room. For Taylor, for Dillon, and for me. Despite the danger I'd put myself in, once again, I knew more than ever this was who I was. A nutty young woman who would risk her own safety to help those who needed her.

39

DILLON

I STOOD OUTSIDE, PRACTICALLY FREEZING MY REAR OFF AS I waited for Selena to arrive at the police station. It had been a few days since the incident, but I was still shaken. I jumped at strange noises and was constantly on guard. I supposed I would be fine inside the station, but somehow the idea of having Selena by my side eased my fears.

When Selena's stepmother had recommended I stay with my parents for a while and see a therapist, I thought she was being an overprotective parent, but she'd been right. There had been comfort in sleeping, or more accurately trying to sleep, in my childhood bedroom knowing my parents were a few doors down. Mom's home-cooked meals and Dad's evening cocktails were something I looked forward to. Being back home was like a haven - safe and warm, unlike my apartment. I don't know if I'd ever return.

As it was, every other image that crossed my mind was of a gun in my face, a gun at Selena's temple, or the image of Taylor turning the weapon on herself. I hadn't been to school or work. Luckily, my professors had been understanding and sent me assignments through email, and my boss told me to take all the time I needed. It had become difficult to leave my parents' house or concentrate or do anything other than eat and drink with my parents. Considering Martina had been right about reaching out to my parents, I still hadn't slept in days, so I took her other advice and made an appointment with a therapist.

I hadn't seen Selena since the event, but I looked forward to it now. It would not be a fun, chatty lunch, rather, it would be us confirming our statements from that night. Now, here I was at the San Francisco Police Department, the first time outside of my parents' house in three days, and I didn't feel safe despite my proximity to law-enforcement.

From across the parking lot, I spotted Selena heading toward me, decked out in a black coat and beanie. My heartbeat quickened when she smiled and waved. She was amazing.

I was excited, but also filled with guilt that I put her in this situation. I should have never told her about my stalker and figured it out on my own. If Taylor had come after me, I could live with that, but if she'd harmed Selena, I don't think I could have. The thought felt like a dagger to my chest. What kind of man couldn't handle a girl who had a crush on them?

Selena approached. "Hi Dillon, how are you?" She said with a hint of apprehension in her voice.

"All right."

She cocked her head. "Yeah?"

"As all right as I can be."

She opened her mouth, presumably to speak, but I raised my hand to stop her. "If it's okay, I wanted to say a few things to you before we go in. Is that okay?"

She nodded.

"I took your advice, and I have an appointment with a thera-pist on Friday. Thank you for saving me and Taylor." I stopped her again before she could talk. "I also wanted to apologize for getting you involved in all of this. I feel terrible and responsible.

You were right, I shouldn't have tried to blow Taylor off. I should have told her I was never interested. It's my fault. I'm so sorry." I looked down at the ground, I couldn't face her with tears in my eyes. I felt her hand on my shoulder.

She moved closer and whispered, "It's not your fault."

I met her gaze. "It is."

She shook her head. "No, it's not your fault at all. If you hadn't asked for my help, who knows what could've happened. If it wasn't me she went after, it could've been the next girl that you dated or spent time with. You did the right thing."

"It doesn't feel that way."

"You have nothing to be sorry about. Trust me, Taylor has issues. This isn't your fault."

"Then, why do I feel so terrible?"

"Because you're human."

My gaze locked with her warm brown eyes. She really was amazing. "You ready to go in?"

"Yep." She said.

I held the door open for her and watched as she walked in. I was still quite attracted to her, but felt too guilty to even have a dirty thought about her.

We sat in a small room with the two officers as we relayed our statements to them, confirming the original, and then signed a form. I set the pen down. "What happened to Taylor, is she in jail?"

Officer Heller explained. "No, she's not in a regular jail. She's in the county mental hospital. We talked to her parents, and they told us her history of mental health issues. They're pretty serious. They hadn't realized she'd gone off her medication, and that she was no longer in therapy. Her mom called her all the time, but according to her mother, Taylor usually just screamed at her and hung up the phone. Her mother said she felt guilty for not realizing she wasn't taking her meds since that type of behavior is consistent with her diagnosis. Who knows, maybe even this situation saved Taylor's life."

I turned to the right and looked at Selena.

She nodded at me with a slight smile.

"Anything else you need from us?"

"No, I think we have it covered. Thank you both for coming down."

Back outside the station, I faced Selena. "I guess this is it."

"We still have class together." She said.

"True, but no more covert operations, I suppose."

She grinned. "I think that's a good thing. But, I'll see you in class, right?"

Although true, my heart sunk. There was still something about Selena that kept her at the top of my mind. "Yeah, I haven't gone all week but plan to go back starting next week."

"I haven't been to class either. Don't rush it if you don't feel ready, it's okay to take as much time as you need."

"Thank you, Selena. Again, I'm sorry."

"Don't be sorry. And you're welcome. I have to run off, but I'll see you next week. You take care." She wrapped her small, powerful arms around me and I did the same. It only lasted a few moments, but I wouldn't ever be able to shake the smell of her melon-scented shampoo from my memory. I waved as she headed toward her car. Damn, I was going to miss her.

40

SELENA

I PUT DOWN MY FORK AFTER INHALING THE TURKEY lasagna my dad had made for dinner. From across the table, Dad chuckled. "So you liked it?"

"Yes, it was fantastic. I think I could eat ten more helpings, but I think I'd explode. You've become quite the home chef."

Martina nodded with a twinkle in her eye. "Yes, he has. I've gained three pounds in the last six months."

I smiled at the thought. Martina wasn't one to break her own protocols. The lasagna was delicious, but fairly healthy, using ground turkey instead of beef. No doubt because of Martina's influence. Martina had subscribed to the 'healthy body, healthy mind' mantra since I'd met her. Dad swallowed his last bite and then wiped his mouth with a paper napkin. "Selena, how is school going? You must be busy, we sure miss you around here."

A side dish of guilt filled me up. "It's pretty good. I have a full load."

"Still on track to graduate this semester?"

"Yep." Even I had a hard time believing that in two-and-a-half months I'd be a college graduate.

Dad smiled from ear to ear. "My daughter, a college graduate and doing it in only three-and-a-half years to boot. I'm so proud of you. I'm so proud of everything you've become. You're tough and smart. You know your mother would have been very proud."

Dad rarely mentioned Mom, at least he hadn't in a few years. The only time we broached the subject was right after we had reconnected and he told me how sorry he was that he had left me behind and that he wasn't proud of himself during those days - when he was an addict. He'd explained he had many regrets, one being how he should've treated Mom and me better. That we deserved better. Mom was far from perfect, but it was true, she deserved better than what she got.

I scooted my chair back and walked over to Dad, who was now tearing up. I wrapped my arms around him, inhaling his spicy cologne. I whispered, "I love you, Dad," in his ear and he returned the sentiment.

I stood back, wiping underneath my eyes with my fingertips. This week had been far too emotional. And it wasn't over yet. I watched Martina who sat silently across the table. I wasn't sure any other person ever had a better stepmother. She had saved me so many times and taught me so many lessons. I walked over and gave her a hug and told her, "Thank you for everything."

She patted me on the back said, "You're very welcome. I love you, Selena."

I mumbled a shaky, "I love you too, Martina," before returning to my chair.

Dad pushed himself up. "There's dessert. I've been trying my hand at baking. I'm not sure if I'll win star baker anytime soon, but I gave it my best shot."

He had my attention now. "What did you make?" Dad knew I had a sweet tooth. It was obvious this dinner had morphed into a celebration, a homecoming of sorts.

"Chocolate-and-raspberry celebration cake."

I grinned. "I can't wait."

"Coffee?" Martina asked.

"Would love some, thank you."

Martina exited, and Dad began clearing the dishes. "Can I help?"

"Oh no, I'll take care of cleanup. And I'll give you and Martina a few minutes to catch up as I put the finishing touches on my chocolate masterpiece."

Apprehension filled my gut, but before I could react, Martina returned with a mug of piping hot coffee. I accepted the mug, donning the Drakos Monroe logo, and took a sip.

Martina reclaimed her seat. "I have a few updates on Taylor."

"Is she doing all right in the hospital?"

"Yes, she's become more stable and is taking her medications regularly. She's asked to see you."

Taylor wanted to see me? I was a little surprised, but wasn't opposed to the idea. She seemed bright and full of life. Someone you'd want to get to know. That was when she wasn't trying to kill you or herself. She seemed like she was someone who needed a friend. "I'd like that. Do you think she'll be in there for a long time?"

"They're trying to put together a deal for her. The judge is looking at her history and the current situation. He'll likely take the recommendation from her psychiatrist to determine the best course of treatment and the amount of time she'll need to be institutionalized."

"I'm glad she's getting the help she needs. Watching her attempt to take her own life was horrifying."

Martina gave a slight nod.

I didn't use terms like horrifying lightly. It had been that bad. I'd seen so many terrible things in my life, but watching someone in so much pain was gut-wrenching. "I don't think I'll ever forget the look in her eyes. The fear, sadness, and loneliness, it was palpable. Even when I feared for my own safety, I felt bad for her."

"That's because you're a good person with lots of empathy for others. I think that's why you're drawn to the more serious investigations. Are you still thinking you want to go out on your own?"

"I think so, but I have a couple of months to decide."

"That you do." Martina stared at her coffee cup for a moment and then looked back at me. "When you go visit Taylor, could you ask her if she would still be willing to sit for a sketch of Kaitlyn's boyfriend? I could go down there myself, but it seems like you've already got a connection with her. Good or bad. We're still hoping that Greg, the boyfriend, is the link to finding Kaitlyn."

I hesitated. "I can definitely ask her, but you don't think Taylor could have anything to do with Kaitlyn's disappearance, do you?"

"Maybe, but I don't think so. When you visit her, if she seems up to it, try questioning her again. See if there are any discrepancies with her previous answers."

I nodded. "When can I see her?"

"You can go tomorrow or wait until Monday. It's up to you. Let me know when you're planning to visit and I'll call ahead to get you credentialed for a visit."

"Thanks, but I can make the arrangements." I looked at Martina, who seemed to hold her breath. She was holding something back. My phone buzzed and I picked it up off the table. I glanced back up at Martina, she said, "Take it."

I answered. "Hello, this is Selena Bailey."

"Hi Selena, this is Detective Brown. How are you doing? I heard you had quite an ordeal this week."

"I'm fine. It all ended up okay. I'm guessing that's not why you called though." I had a sneaking suspicion that Martina knew what the detective was about to tell me.

"No, it's not, but I'm glad you're okay. I wanted you to hear it from me, Honeywell pleaded out. He'll be in prison for twenty years for his role in the trafficking ring."

Before he could continue to speak. I exclaimed, "Only twenty years?"

"It was the deal he made. He gave some sensitive information in exchange for the lighter sentence. "

"What about Brendon's death, did he admit to that?"

"No, he said he wasn't the one who gave the order, and we tend to believe him at this point. We now believe Honeywell isn't the boss and that there's at least two layers above him. It seems Ocampo was pretty low on the food chain - basically, a low level operative. Honeywell was his superior, but he wasn't the one pulling the strings. He likely didn't order Brendon's murder."

I couldn't believe what I was hearing. He'd barely scratched the surface of finding those responsible for who killed Brendon and taking down this particular trafficking ring. "So what's your plan to find the higher-ups?"

I stared at my coffee mug and shoved it away. My body couldn't handle any more jolts to its system.

"Our task force is staying in place. Like I said, Honeywell named some names and we're looking into it. I will keep you updated."

"And that's all you can tell me?"

"That's all I can tell you right now. You have my word, I will keep you updated as we progress."

I shut my eyes and breathed in and out before saying, "Thank you, Detective." And ended the call. I eyed Martina, who sat apprehensively waiting for my reaction. I would not cry. I would not scream. "How long did you know?"

"Someone called me earlier - before dinner. I didn't want to ruin the dinner. Detective Brown said he would call you, and he did. I'll say this one more time, please let the police do their job. They will take care of it. They seem competent enough to build the case against these criminals. They will get justice for Brendon and all the other lives they've ruined."

To date, justice had barely been served. It was more like one itty-bitty bite of a giant justice cookie. I wanted the whole cookie. I wanted them all to pay.

41

SELENA

I WAS ESCORTED BY A LESS-THAN-FRIENDLY SECURITY guard to the visiting room of the county hospital. He opened the door, pointed, and said, "right in there," before sauntering off back down the hall. I entered the large room, which had a sterile vibe but also smelled like sick. I doubt there was any kind of disinfectant that could remove the special mix of sadness and despair. There were tables situated about with, whom I presumed, were patients and visitors. I doubted anyone walked in here wearing pajamas and a bathrobe. The others sat stiffly or clutched their coats. Visitors. Some appeared to be engaged in conversation, whereas others played checkers or cards. Under different circumstances one might have assumed it was a party, but if a celebratory party was bright pink, this was dark gray.

I spotted Taylor sitting by herself at a table with a novel in her hands. Her eyes met mine, and she set the book down on the table. She gave a warm smile, and I approached and sat down across from her. "Hi Taylor, how are you feeling?"

She shrugged. "Fine. My meds kicked in so my insanity has been muted for now."

How does one respond to that? This was far more uncomfortable than I'd expected. "Do you also go to therapy?"

"Oh yeah. They're all about the therapy here. I attend group and one-on-one therapy. It's exhausting."

Ah, an opening. "Tell me about it. I only see my therapist once a week and sometimes that feels like too much."

Taylor's eyes widened just a little. "You have a therapist too?"

"Yep. I started seeing a therapist four years ago after a traumatic experience or two." I chuckled at the irony of the situation. "I saw her three times a week and then dropped to one. I wanted to quit. I felt all talked out, you know? But she convinced me to continue once per week. As much as it feels like work, I know I need it. Not talking about things is rarely the best plan."

Taylor perked up. "Did they give you a diagnosis?"

"Post traumatic stress."

"What happened?"

I sighed. "It's a long story. I could probably fill a novel or two with all my tales."

Her face scrunched up. "Don't like talking about it?"

"Not really."

"I can respect that. I suppose if I were sitting on the other side, I wouldn't want to rehash my past either. I have borderline personality disorder and depression. It's funny, in here everyone shares their diagnosis. It's kind of like in college when everyone asks you what your major is."

"I'm not familiar with that, what's it been like for you?"

"Well, they diagnosed me when I was a sophomore in high school, when my parents sent me to a psychiatrist after finding out I was cutting - self-harming. When I was diagnosed, I felt like a freak or that I was a crazy person, but it was comforting that my wild mood swings and erratic behavior had a name."

She smirked. "Sometimes I'd do things - strange things, but while it was happening, it was as if I'd left my body. I mean, I was in control, but another person takes over. Afterwards, I'm often filled with regret and a sinking feeling that I'd lost control over myself. I've done stupid, really stupid things, as you know."

The sadness in her voice broke my heart. "It sounds scary."

"Yeah, it's no fun fearing your own self and not being able to trust that you know what your next move is going to be. Like what I did to you and Dillon. I can't believe I did that - it's so awful. I never want to be that person again. That is why I wanted you to visit so that I could apologize to you in person. I want to own what I did. I vandalized your car, left threatening notes, and put a gun to your head." She shook her head back and forth as tears escaped. "I wish there were something that I could do to make it up to you and to Dillon."

"Well, I appreciate your apology and I accept it. I just hope that you continue to get help and feel better. We don't always get dealt a fair hand."

"Tell me about it. All I've ever wanted to do was be normal. To be like other people and be able to control my emotions. I want to be happy and functioning."

It wasn't fair. It wasn't like Taylor had a choice to have a mental illness, and society didn't make it any easier with all the stigma and misinformation about mental health issues. Maybe if people understood that mental illness was nothing to be ashamed of, those who needed help wouldn't be afraid to seek it. It could save them and the people who may be harmed by it as well. It was strange, but with Taylor, I felt like I had a strange connection to her even though she *kinda* tried to kill me. But here she was, simply another human being who was lonely and hurting.

"What are you reading?"

"Dean Koontz. He's my new favorite. I used to read a lot of

romance novels, but thought maybe I'd try something new. It's dark, but I'm hooked. I've had a lot of time to read since I've been locked up - so it's not all bad, I guess."

"Maybe I'll check it out." My mind was racing trying to come up with more small talk, but I decided to go with one of my main purposes for visiting. "Oh, I almost forgot. We missed your appointment with the sketch artist. Are you still up for the challenge?"

Taylor nodded. "Of course. Kaitlyn was the only real friend I ever had until Greg showed up." She shook her head. "I can't believe she's still missing. I have a bad feeling, you know? Like maybe I'll never be able to tell her how much she meant to me."

I had a bad feeling that she wouldn't either. "I know this is last minute, but we arranged for a sketch artist to come here today. Are you okay with that?"

"Absolutely. Anything I can do to help find Kaitlyn."

"I'm going to call her, she's close by." I pushed off my seat and walked back through the double doors and called the sketch artist, gave her the details and returned to Taylor.

While we waited, I re-questioned Taylor about Kaitlyn, her last conversation, and the last time she'd seen her. It was all consistent. My gut told me Taylor had nothing to do with her friend's disappearance.

Twenty minutes later, the sketch artist that the firm used rather regularly approached us. I introduced the two and scooted away so that they could get to work.

I watched as Taylor described features to Stacy, the artist, as she furiously sketched, often asking "like this or more like this?" At the end, a man with dark hair and sharp features stared back from the page. It was fascinating. Stacy patted Taylor on the shoulder. "Great work."

"Thanks."

Stacy turned to me and said, "I'll bring this back to Martina. Anything else you want me to relay to her?"

"Tell her we don't have any additional information."

"You got it. I'll see you. Taylor, you take care."

She waved before exiting. I thought it might be a good time to do the same. I was halfway out of my chair when Taylor said, "Can I ask you something, Selena?"

I sat back down. "Sure, what is it?"

"I probably shouldn't be asking, but despite my terrible actions, I did care for Dillon. Is he okay?"

I wasn't sure how much Dillon would want me to share. "Dillon will be okay." He would be in time.

"Some other patients in here were telling me that what I did to him could scar him for life. That makes me feel sick. It's the last thing I wanted for him. I never wanted to hurt him or anyone. If you can, please tell him I'm sorry. I really mean it. I promise not to reach out to him again."

"Of course."

"I suppose now you two can be an item for real."

My mouth dropped open. What? Sure, I'd thought he was cute and all, and he had that certain something, but I still wasn't convinced I was ready to date.

"Come on, you must see the way he looks at you."

"What do you mean?"

"Look, I'm not saying that the two of you were dating, but there's definitely sparks between you. It drove me mad. You should go for it. You both deserve to be happy."

Of all the odd things Taylor had done, this seemed to take the cake. I shook my head. "Oh, I don't know. I should really get going. I have another appointment." It was a lie, but I wasn't sure I could do this dance anymore, not today. I stood up. "It was good to see you, Taylor. Take care of yourself."

"Thank you, Selena. You can visit anytime, you know — in

the event you get the inclination to want to visit a crazy person. I have a feeling I'll be here for a while." She chuckled lightly.

At least she had a sense of humor about it. Sometimes laughter was the most effective medicine. I said, "Will do." And who knows, I just might.

I exited through the double doors of the county hospital visiting zone. I was glad to be gone; I imagined it was probably only slightly better than an actual prison. At least Taylor was getting help, and that was something. And fingers crossed that Taylor's sketch would help us find Kaitlyn.

42

SELENA

I set my toasted sesame bagel with cream cheese down and finished chewing before I gazed across the table at Dillon, whose dimples were on full display as he smiled at me. He was obviously pleased that I had accepted his invitation to have coffee before class today. It was his first day back after being held hostage. He looked well. His hair was shiny. His eyes were bright, and he was clean-shaven. He certainly was easy on the eyes. Was Taylor right? Did he have a thing for me? We seemed to have a connection. Was that a good thing? "Do you feel ready to be back at school?"

"I'm definitely ready for some form of normalcy. I'm still staying at my parents' house and commuting in, but it feels good to be back. What a rollercoaster the last few weeks have been. I don't know how I would've gotten through it without you and your stepmother. Please thank her for me. I don't think I would have thought to stay with my parents or gone to see a counselor if she hadn't practically commanded me to do so."

I chuckled. "Martina has that effect on people. She's pretty no-nonsense. I'll relay the message."

"Thanks. How about you? I'm not the only one who was held hostage. How have you been?"

"I'm okay. Sleep isn't something I'm doing as much as I should, but I've never been a good sleeper. I've always been on edge or worried something may go bump in the night. I have a regular therapist that I see. I know this is temporary. I'll be fine."

"How long have you seen this therapist? Does it really help?"

"It does. It's not always easy, but it has helped me get through some rough times. How are your sessions going?"

"Pretty good, I've gone a few times. I think its helping. My therapist also gave me something to help me sleep. It's temporary, just so I can get my energy back up in order for me to finish up school, study for the LSAT and then apply to law schools."

He was smart too. Not that I'd denied being drawn to him, I just wasn't totally sure I was ready. "What are your top choices?"

His eyes lit up. "I have a huge list. At the top are Harvard, Yale, UC Berkeley, and Golden Gate University. I'll need a mix of luck and high LSATs to be accepted."

"I'm sure you'll get in. Do you still want to be an entertainment lawyer?"

He nodded. "That's the plan for now. Although this experience has opened up my eyes to other potential areas of law I could get into."

"I suppose you don't have to decide right away, you still have time."

"I do. How about you? What do you plan to do after graduation - which for you is pretty soon? Are you pretty stoked?"

"I plan to stay in private investigations, and I'm about 95% sure I will start my own firm instead of staying at Drakos Monroe." In my mind I had made my decision but was having a troublesome time speaking the words. Was it because then it would be true?

"Why would you leave?"

It wasn't a terrible question. Drakos Monroe was one of the top security and investigations firms in the entire San Francisco Bay Area. They had all the resources and all the top personnel. They also had all the rules. Rules I didn't like. "I don't know if it's a good fit right now. I like it there and everything, but there are a few too many rules for my liking."

"I could see that." His smile was replaced with a somber look. "So one reason I wanted to meet with you was to thank you - again. But also I've had a lot of time to think. A lot of my thoughts drifted to you and the time we spent working together on the KT case. I missed talking to you and seeing you. I think you're really spectacular and I just wondered if you might want to hang out without a dangerous stalker after us?" He laughed nervously.

Taylor had been right. There had been sparks between Dillon and me. As Dillon wore his heart on his sleeve, I kept mine closer to the chest. Was I really ready for this? My track record with dating was nothing short of terrible. My first boyfriend tried to kill me and I got the second one killed. What would happen to a third? Literally, all of my boyfriends were dead. *Yikes.* Was my fate to walk this life alone?

Maybe I should take Dee's advice and just date casually, or at least give it a shot. It wasn't like every man I dated had to turn into a boyfriend. Maybe it would be fun. Dee was brave enough to date again. Maybe I should be too. Boy, had Dee gotten in my head. She had me back in the gym and now this.

"I'm not opposed to that. Did you have anything specific in mind?"

His dimples returned, and I knew it was the right decision. He said, "Well, there's a new movie out that the critics are raving about. Friday is opening night. Would you like to join me? Maybe we could do dinner after?"

Dinner and a movie. It didn't get more normal than that. "I'd like that." We continued to discuss movies as we finished our bagels and coffee before heading to class. I hadn't mentioned my visit with Taylor in fear that our very normal conversation would turn into a drama instead of a light romantic comedy. Because in these moments, it was almost as if I was a normal girl. *Go figure.*

43

SELENA

I stood against the wall and watched as Dee sat perched on the edge of my bed, describing her dates with the new guy. She wore a smile and bright eyes. She was clearly smitten with him. If there was hope for Dee, maybe there was hope for me too. I grinned as she swooned and laid back on the bed with her hand over her heart. "He just makes me feel so warm and tingly." She sat back up. "Does that make me sound silly?"

"No, it's sweet. You like him and I'm so happy for you."

"I'm happy for me too, and I'm happy for you going on your first date since..." Dee paused. "A long time."

Those around me knew better than to mention Brendon's name. When I heard it or read it, the ache in my heart throbbed. I couldn't even bring myself to say his name. I sighed. "Yeah, I guess I'm ready to try." I did like Dillon, but I don't know if it would last a date or a year. My therapist explained I couldn't control everything in my life and encouraged me to go on the date with Dillon and to take it one day at a time without worrying about what the future may hold.

Dee situated herself into a cross-legged position. "Okay, tell me everything about Dillon."

"He's really cute, and he's smart. He's really into movies and wants to go to law school."

Dee eyed me. "Okay, that's his resume. What do you like about him?"

"He's easy to talk to. I don't know, we get a long. I like hanging out with him."

"That's a start." Dee looked me up and down.

"What?"

"You're going to wear that?"

I glanced down at my outfit. Black jeans, black top, and black boots. I looked back up at her. "What's wrong with what I'm wearing?"

"Nothing. I think you should express yourself however you want to express yourself. If you're comfortable, that's great, but it's what you usually wear to school, right? And this is a date."

She had a point. "What do you think I should wear? This is what most of my wardrobe looks like, but I may have something that's a little more lively, like a sweater."

"Oh, c'mon. We lived together, I know you own all kinds of brightly colored clothes. You must have some of them left."

Before I could say anything, Dee was off the bed rummaging through my closet. Dee called out, "aha," and then pulled out a white flowing blouse.

I hadn't worn the piece since freshman year. "You think that's good for a date?"

"Yes. That with a red scarf will be perfect. And the best part is you can still wear your black jeans and boots. You'll still be you, but with some flare. Plus, your skin looks great against the crisp white, you'll glow like a beautiful angel."

We both laughed at the ridiculous comment. "Perfect. That

was exactly the look I was going for." I chuckled. "No, seriously, thank you for coming over. I appreciate it."

"Anytime. Look at us, two dating ladies. Who would've ever thought we'd be here again?"

I scoffed. "Not me."

"Me neither."

My phone vibrated on my nightstand. Dee ran over and said, "Martina's calling you."

A bit of relief fell over me. I half thought maybe Dillon was calling to tell me he had changed his mind and that he couldn't make it for our date. In that moment, I knew I really wanted to go out with him. I answered. "Hi Martina. Are we still on for dinner on Sunday night?" I was happy that Dad and Martina convinced me to do a Sunday night dinner every week. It would keep us connected and I'd really missed being in their home surrounded by their warmth. "Yes, does Sunday at five work for you?"

"Sunday at five is perfect."

"You sound cheerful."

I suppose I couldn't hide my excitement. "Dee came over to help me get ready for my date."

"A date? Is it with Dillon?"

Did everybody see the sparks between Dillon and I? "Yep, it's with Dillon. We're going to a movie and then dinner."

"That sounds great. I hope you have a good time. But, actually, the reason I'm calling is that we have some news."

A sour feeling filled my gut. "What is it?"

"Based on the sketch Taylor helped with, we located Kaitlyn's boyfriend. We shared the information with the police, who then allowed us to go with them when they questioned him. Taylor had been right. He was not a good guy. He was the worst kind of guy. It was what we feared."

It made me sick to think there were so many abusers out

there. "What happened when you questioned him?" I sat myself down on the bed and cringed at Dee.

"We arrived at his apartment, Kaitlyn wasn't there, but another young woman was. She was covered in bruises. We separated them and were able to question her alone. We were able to get the woman to talk. She explained that she was terrified of Greg because he told her if she didn't do what he told her to he would do to her what he had done to his last girlfriend. She said she didn't know what happened to Kaitlyn because the only time Greg mentioned her was when he was threatening her. She wanted to leave him, but was too scared to go through with it."

"That's awful. Did you find Kaitlyn?"

"The detectives found drugs in the apartment and were able to arrest Greg. After they got him back to the station, they went at him hard and he confessed to murdering her in exchange for a lesser sentence. They found Kaitlyn buried in a shallow grave out on the Delta. From the preliminary assessment, Kaitlyn was likely killed shortly after her graduation."

My heart sunk. Another woman who lost her life to an abusive man. A victim instead of a survivor. "Thanks for letting me know. Part of me knew that was the most likely scenario. I wish I'd been wrong. At least we can bring closure to Kaitlyn's family. Have you told Taylor?"

"Not yet. I was wondering if you maybe wanted to tell her."

Want to tell her? *No.* I never wanted to have to give a death notification to a friend or family member. Taylor would be crushed. "I can do that. Taylor said they were best friends and that their only falling out was over Greg, because she didn't approve of him."

"Too bad Taylor didn't tell anybody about her concerns earlier, but she couldn't have known that it could lead to her death. In the end, it was because of Taylor we were able to find Kaitlyn. She should be proud of herself, please tell her that."

Another tragedy. "Okay, I will. Thanks for letting me know. I'll see you Sunday." I hung up and looked over at Dee.

She frowned. "What is it?"

I explained Kaitlyn's story to Dee and the connection to Taylor.

Dee's mouth dropped open. "You know, maybe all of this stuff with Taylor happened for a reason. If Taylor had never stalked Dillon and Dillon hadn't sought your help with Taylor, Taylor wouldn't have tried to talk to you and you wouldn't have found the connection between her and Kaitlyn. It's because of this whole KT thing that they were able to find Kaitlyn. Kinda crazy, right?"

I hadn't thought of it that way. Taylor had been the key to finding Kaitlyn. If it wasn't for Taylor, I wouldn't be going on my first date in a year-and-a-half either. It was funny how things turned out sometimes.

I changed into the top Dee had suggested and checked out my reflection. It brightened up my look quite a bit. I now looked like I was going on a date and less like I was going to a funeral. I turned around to Dee. "I suppose its time."

"Is he picking up or are you meeting at the theater?"

"We're meeting at the theater."

"Well, my dear. Good luck."

I gave a nervous grin. "Thanks." I had a feeling I needed it.

44

SELENA

THREE MONTHS LATER

I stepped forward and then stopped to read the nameplate next to the door. I smiled widely as I pulled out the key from my pocket. The key that Martina had so lovingly gift-wrapped and handed to me on the day of my college graduation. My mind drifted back to that day.

I stood before Dad, Martina, Zoey, Dee and Dillon. Martina said, "Congratulations on your graduation, Selena. Your dad and I got you something." She then handed me a small white box with a red ribbon tied into a bow.

I undid the bow and lifted the lid which revealed a set of silver keys. I didn't understand the significance. "What do they open?"

Dad and Martina exchanged glances. Martina explained. "Those keys open the door to the Bailey Investigations office - your new office. Your dad and I have pre-paid a one-year lease for a small office downtown. It's for you, Selena, for when you start your investigations firm. The space is in an office park with storefronts that are known for walk-in traffic, plus you'll be only a block away from Drakos Monroe so you and I could have lunch together or discuss cases - that is if you wanted to."

I didn't even try to fight the tears, and neither did Martina, who is normally quite stoic. I wrapped one arm around Martina and the other around Dad. I don't know how long it was before I let go of them. At that moment, I felt like the luckiest person alive.

GRADUATION HAD BEEN A GREAT DAY. I WORE THE DORKY black cap and gown, taking silly and serious photos with Dad, Martina, and Zoey before launching into a photoshoot with Dee and a few with Dillon. It was such a joyful day, but even with the happiness, there had still been a cloud. Brendon should've been there and my mom too. It wasn't fair they weren't there physically, but I could feel them in my heart and knew that they were there cheering me on with the rest of my family and friends. Maybe it was silly, but I swear I could.

I inserted the key into the lock on the door and turned the knob. I pushed the door open and stepped into the office for my first day as a private investigator and small business owner. I held my breath as I surveyed the office.

It was just how Martina and I had set it up. Not only had Martina and Dad paid for the lease, but they also helped me pick out furniture to set up the office. Martina didn't tell Dad, but she also used her powers of influence so that Drakos Monroe would send any overflow traffic to me and my new company. I know that few people were as lucky as I was. It was hard starting your own business, but the fact that Dad and Martina believed in me helped build my confidence that I could make Bailey Investigations a success.

I believed in me too.

I knew I could do this. I knew I could help other people and make a living while I was at it. I'd even drafted a five-year business plan in order to set my future straight. To be fair, it had also been an assignment for one of my classes, but either way I had it and I intended to follow it.

I set my backpack down, took off my coat, and hung it on the coat rack that Martina insisted I needed. I pulled out the chair, sat down and surveyed the small office. It was 200 ft.^{2} and it was all mine. I had a desk, chairs, and a filing cabinet. I even had a tiny little nook for my coffee maker. The only window was on the door with views to the parking lot, but that was okay. I had plenty of lighting, albeit artificial. It didn't matter; it was the best 200 ft.^{2} I'd ever been in.

I powered up my computer and opened up my e-mail. Before reading any messages, I glanced at my desk and straightened my business card holder that held my brand-new business cards. They read Bailey Investigations in black block lettering with my new business phone number, email, and website at the bottom on a bright white background. I had the office, the business cards, and now all I needed were some clients.

I refocused on my inbox. There were no messages pertaining to investigations, but I stopped scrolling when I saw an email from Dillon. I smiled as I drafted a reply expressing congratulations for being admitted into law school. I was glad he still felt comfortable sharing the news since we'd broken up only a few weeks ago. *On Christmas.* I know, it was terrible timing, but he had decided that was the day that he wanted to tell me he loved me. A gift of sorts. Except, when he said it, my fight-or-flight impulses kicked in and I wanted to run away. I figured that was as good a sign as any that I wasn't in love with him. I knew what it felt like to love, and this just wasn't it. I had fun going to movies and hanging out with Dillon. It was all so easy and carefree, but I knew it wasn't serious. Dillon didn't. I took my own advice and told him the truth. It was your standard, "I think you're a great guy, but I don't feel the same way, can we still be friends?" It was sucky, but it was honest.

After I clicked send, a new email message from Martina popped up.

Hi Selena,

I have a potential client here who needs help with a background check for their small business. Do you have any time to take the assignment? We're swamped here. Let me know and I'll forward your contact information to the client.

Best,

Martina

I began tapping on my keyboard.

Hi Martina,

Thank you for the referral. Yes, I have some time to help out the client.

Thank you,

Selena Bailey

Bailey Investigations

I hit send and sat back in my chair. I was fairly certain Drakos Monroe could handle a simple background check for a small firm. I had a sneaking suspicion Martina was giving me a 'first day on the job' present. I usually regarded background checks as terribly boring, but considering it would be for my first client, I was super excited. I had half a mind to cover up the window, turn on the music, and dance around the small office. I was so freaking excited. I couldn't remember the last time I was this excited.

My phone buzzed on my new Bailey Investigations line. I thought it must be the background check client. I cleared my throat and sat up straight. "Bailey Investigations, how may I help you?"

"Is this Selena Bailey?"

I wanted to have an air of professionalism, but there was no way I was near having a receptionist and didn't feel I needed to pretend. "This is Selena Bailey, how may I help you?"

"My name is Vicky Crawford, I was referred to you by a mutual friend, Dee Hankel. She says you may be able to help."

Not the background check client. A second client? I tried to contain my giddiness. "What can I help you with?"

"It's my sister, Stephanie. She was found unconscious in her apartment. She's in the hospital and they don't know why she is so sick. They're running tests, but I have my suspicions, but the police won't take them seriously. I think she's sick because of some bad medication given to her by a shady doctor."

Hmm. I wasn't sure how I could help investigate pharmaceuticals, but a shady doctor, I could be all over that. "Why don't you start from the beginning and tell me why you're suspicious of this doctor."

"It started a few months back. Stephanie began seeing a doctor to help her lose weight. He swore to her he had miracle methods to make her beautiful. I didn't buy it from the start, but she always thought she needed to lose weight. This guy said he could make her thin. I tried to warn her that he was no good but when she started shedding pounds fast - too fast — Stephanie said it was proof the doctor was legit. She said he gave her vitamins to help her with her diet, but I'm not sure that is all. It just didn't add up. In the last month, she's lost an alarming amount of weight and has seemingly fallen under this doctor's spell. Last night she collapsed and is now in the intensive care unit. I know he must have given her something. Something dangerous.

I want to know who he is and what he's doing so we can save my sister. The police are refusing to look into this. We need someone to investigate this doctor and see what is really going on with him and his patients. Dee said you might be a great fit because you could probably go undercover, being a young woman yourself, and that you're a fantastic investigator. Do you think you can help? If so, are you available to start immediately?"

If Dee wasn't in class right now, I'd run to her and give her the biggest bear-hug of my life. That would have to wait until she was out of class and, of course, I was done with work for the day. After all, I had a business to run. I smiled. "Yes, I think I can help and yes, I can start immediately." I continued to ask questions and type notes into my computer. My mind was racing with different avenues I could pursue to find out what was causing my client's sister's illness. I would help her. I would save the sister, because... I looked up and out my window... it's what I do. I'm Selena Bailey, Private Investigator.

A NOTE FROM H.K. CHRISTIE

Dear readers,

I hope you enjoyed *Go With Grace*. Over the years, I've known many, myself included, who have struggled with mental health - in varying degrees. However, one thing that has been a consistent theme, in my experience, is the stigma or pushback for seeking help from a trained professional. Whether it is an issue of the expense or the attitude that 'people in our family don't go to therapists' or society who are quick to judge or call someone 'crazy' I think it is preventing people from getting the help they need. I'm not an expert on the subject of mental health, but I hoped with writing *Go With Grace* it would shine a light on the fact that there is NO SHAME in seeking help for a mental health issue or taking medication if it's needed. Be kind to yourself and to others.

Best wishes for health, wealth, opportunity and happiness.
H.K. Christie

(From: mentalhealthfirstaid.org)

If you or someone you know is considering suicide,

**call 9-1-1 or the National Suicide Prevention Life-
line at 1-800-273-TALK (8255).**

When you're trying to find mental health information and
support, it can be overwhelming and hard to know where to
start. A simple Google search of the term "mental health" alone
will give you more than 1.9 million results.

Although sometimes it can be hard to find, trustworthy and
reliable support is out there and can help you and your loved
ones get the information you need.

**These five mental health resources can #BeThe-
Difference when you need it most.**

1 The National Suicide Prevention Line. This hotline
provides free, confidential support 24/7 to people in distress
across the United States. Call 1-800-273-TALK (8255) for
support.

2 The SAMHSA Helpline. SAMHSA's National Helpline
is a free, confidential information service that provides treatment and support referrals 24/7 to people facing mental illness
and addictions. Call 1-800-662-HELP (4357) for support.

3 Crisis Text Line. Crisis Text Line provides free, confidential support via text message 24/7 to those in crisis situations.
Text HOME to 741741 for support.

4 The Trevor Project. The Trevor Project provides free,
confidential support 24/7 to LGBTQ youth via a helpline, text
and online instant messaging system. Call 1-866-488-7386 for
support.

5 The Veterans Crisis Line. The Veterans Crisis line
provides free, confidential support 24/7 to veterans, all service
members and their family and friends in times of need. Call 1-
800-273-8255 and press 1 or text 838255 for support.

ALSO BY H.K. CHRISTIE

For a full list of books by H.K. Christie, please go to your favorite retailer or visit

authorhkchristie.com

THANK YOU!

Thank you for reading *Go With Grace*! I hope you enjoyed reading it as much as I loved writing it. If you did, I would greatly appreciate if you could post a short review.

Reviews are crucial for any author and can make a huge difference in visibility of current and future works. Reviews allow us to continue doing what we love, *writing stories*. Not to mention, I would be forever grateful!

Thank you!

JOIN H.K. CHRISTIE'S READER CLUB

Join my reader club to be the first to hear about upcoming novels, new releases, giveaways, promotions, as well as, a free e-copy of the Martina Monroe Thriller, *Crashing Down*.

It's completely free to sign up and you'll never be spammed by me, you can opt out easily at any time.

Sign up today
authorhkchristie.com

ABOUT THE AUTHOR

H.K. Christie is the author of compelling stories about unbreakable women.

When not working on her latest novel, she can be found eating, drinking, running slowly, or playing with her favorite furry pal.

She is a native and current resident of the San Francisco Bay Area.

www.authorhkchristie.com

ACKNOWLEDGMENTS

The Selena Bailey series has been a passion project for me. I fell in love with Selena's character and the ability to bring awareness of real-world issues while entertaining. So I want to extend many thanks to all the people who have contributor to the series: my ARC team, my Betas, my editors, and my cover artist. I couldn't have brought Selena to life without all of you.

Made in the USA
Coppell, TX
01 July 2022

79441227R00132